Red-Line Blues

Red-Line Blues

Camilla Reghelini Rivers

James Lorimer & Company Ltd., Publishers
Toronto, 2002

James Lorimer & Company Ltd. acknowledges the support of the Ontario Arts Council. We acknowledge the support of the Government of Canada through the Book Publishing Industry Development Program (BPIDP) for our publishing activities. We acknowledge the support of the Canada Council for the Arts for our publishing program.

Cover illustration: Cam Wilson

Canada Cataloguing in Publication Data

Rivers, Camilla Reghelini
   Red-line blues / Camilla Reghelini Rivers

(Sports stories series)
ISBN 1-55028-828-8 (bound)   ISBN 1-55028-781-8 (pbk.)

I. Title. II. Series: Sports stories (Toronto, Ont.)

PS8585.I8776R43 2002   jC813'.6   C2002-904809-5
PZ7

James Lorimer & Company Ltd., Distributed in the United States by:
Publishers   Orca Book Publishers
35 Britain Street   P.O. Box 468
Toronto, Ontario   Custer, WA USA
M5A 1R7   98240-0468
www.lorimer.ca

Printed and bound in Canada.

Contents

Dedicated to Ron and his Uncles

Gus, for his desire to play being greater than his desire for fame;

Romie, for his humility;

and Joe for being content to stand in the shadows

of his younger brothers

Special thanks to Washmakwa Jerod White

Introduction

Though the story and characters in *Red-Line Blues* are fictitious, Uncles Gus, Romie and Joe did exist. The three brothers played hockey in the 1920s and 1930s and were quite well known in Winnipeg. They were all offered NHL contracts but Gus was the only one that chose to turn pro. Joe and Romie made names for themselves by playing on amateur teams that won the Allen Cup and the World Cup. Romie was also on the1932 Olympic Team that won the gold medal.

The excerpts in italics are from actual newspaper clippings and letters from Romie and Joe while playing in the World Cup. The letters from Gus to his older brother Stan, on the other hand, are a dramatization of Gus' journey as a professional player.

Prologue

When I think back, I realize that it all started that Sunday afternoon last April when Grandpa let me rifle through the stuff in Uncle Joe's cedar chest. There were photos, birth certificates, report cards, letters and scrapbooks full of newspaper clippings. Gold, pure gold. But best of all I had books — real sports books — with their names in them. I knew then that the family history project Ms. Fonseca gave us was going to be a cinch, but I never guessed the importance of that moment.

All my life I'd heard stories about The Uncles. Until then that's all they were — stories. Even the jerseys and trophies, wonderful as they are, never seemed attached to anyone real. But all around me lay the bits and pieces of their lives proving that they were living, breathing, people. I belonged to these men as surely as I belonged to my grandpa or dad. They smiled back at me from the black and white photos with my own smile. There was no doubt these were my ancestors.

THE PORT ARTHUR NEWS-CHRONICLE — 1931
FAMOUS BROTHERS HERE
Romeo Rivers, member of the Winnipeg hockey team which won the Allen Cup this year, and Gus Rivers, member of the Cana-

diens hockey team which won the Stanley Cup, arrived in the city this afternoon by automobile from Winnipeg. They will spend the weekend with their brother Stanley...

1

Answering the Call

FREE PRESS EVENING BULLETIN
POPULAR ATHLETE JOINS PRO. RANKS
Winnipeg, Thursday, January 23, 1930
By Edward Armstrong
...Another of Winnipeg's hockey luminaries has received and answered the call of the major league moguls... Gus Rivers left this morning for Montreal, where he will immediately join the Canadiens, better known as the "Flying Frenchmen."

January 20, 1930
Dear Stan,
Congratulate the newest Montreal Canadien. After a lot of discussion Cecil Hart's agent Tony Gingras finally agreed to my price of five grand a year, for two years. Detroit could only offer four and Chicago couldn't match it either. Thank heaven that's over — I hate all the secrecy. You know how good I am at keeping my trap shut...

Gus

P.S. Keep this letter in a safe place — my signature might be worth something one of these days. Ha. Ha.

The ghosts of my uncles haunt me. They invade my thoughts when I least expect it. Everywhere I turn in Grandpa's house there are things that belonged to them — mugs, medals and trophies. There's enough stuff that we could create a museum if we put them all together in one place. A museum in honour of the Rivers Brothers, Winnipeg hockey heroes of the 1930s. Between them they've won all the big ones — Stanley Cup, World Cup and Olympic gold. As you can guess, they aren't actually my uncles. They are my grandfather's. That makes them my great-grand-uncles, or something, but I've always known them as Uncles Gus, Romie, and Joe.

After I presented my family history project for language arts last April, Ryan Thunderchild took to stalking me. He was a big, quiet kid that had come to our school from The Pas in January. He hardly ever smiled. A shadow of a frown seemed to always crease his forehead. At first I thought he was worried about being the new kid on the block, but when we tried to include him in things, like going to the movies or bowling, he always said no. We finally gave up and he took to hanging with the troublemakers — when he hung with anyone.

"Rivers," he called, blocking me from leaving school that afternoon.

"GET OUT OF MY WAY." I tried to push past him before he could do or say anything.

He stood firm and silent for a moment, then shook his head and said, "Who would have thunk it — with such a gene pool one could end up with a *Puff*?"

"That's Lee to you," I snapped, sick of people calling me Puff or Wheezy. Some kid had tagged me with them because of my asthma and now everyone felt free to use the nicknames.

"You mean *Stan...ley*?" He said my name as if it was some kind of joke. Then he doubled over laughing. "Holy moley, I just figured it out. They named you after the flipping cup."

"Knock it off, you creep. For your information, I'm named after my great-grandfather." I pushed past him.

From that moment on I was no longer happy playing road hockey or fooling around on the rink that Dad built each winter — I wanted to play for a team. And, from that moment on my uncles started haunting me.

Now my mind rings with "Why not you? It's in your blood. Go ahead. Give it a try."

Yeah, why not me? Since The Uncles, no one in the family has played hockey seriously. They say that talent skips a generation — so, why not two? Can't I be the next great Rivers?

I take a deep breath. Here goes.

"I'd like to sign up for hockey at the community club this winter." I steel myself for the objections. It costs too much. The time commitment is too great. What about your asthma?

Mom and Dad look at each other across the kitchen table and shrug.

"It's okay by me. What do you think, dear?" Dad forks up a mouthful of chicken.

"Sure. Why not?" Mom pushes her unruly blond curls off her face. "You know, you might not be with your friends. They've been playing for years."

"I know. I just want to give it a try, that's all."

"What do you say I call the club to find out the particulars? Eh, bud?" Dad reaches over and ruffles my hair.

* * *

Dad and I stand in the hockey registration line. It snakes around the John Forsyth Community Club's gym encircling the shorter queues for the other winter activities. The room is a buzz of sound. Kids are yelling to each other as they dart in and out, between the adults. A few call out to me and I wave back silently. I don't want anyone to invade my special moment of picking up the torch from The Uncles.

"Why so quiet?" Dad rakes his thick dark hair with his spidery fingers.

How can I explain the importance of this to anyone? Especially Dad — he gave up on community club sports when he was my age.

We inch forward. The column splits into several shorter lines and Dad moves into the atom division queue.

I feel a light tap on my back.

"Is this the line for eleven-year-olds?"

I turn to face the source of the squeaky voice. He's tiny, barely up to my shoulder, and skinny, too.

"Yeah," I answer.

"Great." His blue eyes twinkle behind his gold-rimmed glasses. "I'm Scott Kessle."

I resent the intrusion, so I don't respond. That doesn't stop him, though.

"Just moved into the area. I don't know too many kids yet. Figured this would help." He waves his bony hands at the registration table. "Bye," he calls as I follow Dad to the cashier's table.

I anxiously wait as Dad gives her the forms and makes out the cheque to pay for the registration. When she hands him the receipt, I let the air woosh out of my lungs — it's official — I'm playing hockey.

"Thank heaven that's done. Who would have thought it would take this long?" Dad replaces his wallet into his jacket pocket and strides toward the door.

A cinnamon hand reaches out from the crowd and stops me. Ryan.

"Take your hand off me, Thunderchild." I wrench my arm free.

His brown eyes harden. "Saw you sign up for hockey, Puff. Your ancestors must be squirming in their graves."

Jerk. What business is it of his?

"What was that about?" Dad asks.

"Nothing," I mumble.

As we drive home Dad rambles on about his one and only venture into organized hockey.

"It was crazy. Two practices and a game each week. That is, if they hadn't signed us up for tournaments. Then the whole family had to eat, drink and breathe hockey for the duration. There must have been one every other weekend. Between that, school and music practice there wasn't time for much else. What kind of a life was that for a kid? I smartened up fast. Called it quits at the end of the season."

Mom is waiting at the door with a million questions. Talk to anyone interesting? When will we know about the teams? What equipment do we need to buy?

I leave them in the family room, drinking coffee and discussing the advantages of buying second-hand stuff compared with new.

* * *

We've just finished Sunday dinner. The adults are lingering over their tea around Grandpa's kitchen table. They're loudly discussing something the government's done. I head for the quiet of the den. Uncle Joe's old cedar chest draws me to it. I stroke the warm wood, all amber and gold. The top surface is marred by a couple of white water spots — drinks spilled and left to stain by careless children. Plunking myself on the sofa, I lift the lid. The faint smell of bay leaf assaults my nostrils. Grandpa says it was used in the olden days to protect things from insect damage. The chest is filled with old papers, letters and photos. The first time Grandpa let me rummage through them was for my project. I'd never wanted to before because all the really good stuff, like the gold medals and sweaters, are framed and on display around his house. A black and white portrait of Uncle Romie is on the top. He smiles back at me. His eyes twinkle, as if to say, "Atta boy. You'll do us proud."

I sift through the contents. From the pile of snapshots I pull out a number and spread them on the seat beside me. I think they're of The Uncles. I can see the family resemblance. Dad is built like Uncle Joe — slim and tall. I figure I'm more like Uncles Romie and Gus. It's not that we're short but we're definitely boxy. Mom calls it barrel chested and big boned. Dad likes to tease me, saying I bulked up only because of the steroids I take when my asthma is really bad.

"Hey, bud. Come see what I've got." Grandpa slams the basement door shut. On the floor of the hall is an ancient red hockey bag. "It's your dad's stuff from when he was a kid. I figured if you could use any of this, it would save a few bucks."

"Especially if you take after your dad and quit at the end of the season." Mom gives Dad a hip check as he passes her. She's always playing like that. It surprises me how a tiny birdlike creature like my mom can send us flying when she wants to. Low centre of gravity, Dad says.

I drag the bag into the den.

"Don't know how good any of this is, after all the equipment's old." Dad slouches against the door jam, watching me pull out the gear.

"Most of this looks brand new."

"Like I said, it didn't get much use." Mom's green eyes sparkle as she laughs.

I hold up the hockey pants. They look like they'd fit. I grab the skates.

"Oh, wow. They're signed by Gordie Howe!"

"Don't get too excited, sport, that's not an autograph. That model of skate all had his signature stamped on them." Dad chuckles.

"I don't care. If they fit, they're mine." I loosen the laces and pull them on. They fit perfectly. It's an omen. The Great One's skates fit, so, it's got to be a great year. Right?

I try to squeeze my head into the helmet. I can't do it. I have a big head — just like Uncle Romie's.

"We'll have to buy another, Dad. Maybe there'll be a second-hand one at Sport Exchange."

"Wouldn't matter if there was. This is the one thing we will be buying new, for sure." My father raps his knuckles on the helmet as it sits perched like a crown on my head. "There's no way of knowing what kind of knocks and bumps a used one has taken. We want to protect that noggin of yours — even if there's not much there."

In the bottom of the bag is a rumpled red sweater with blue and white stripes.

"So, that's where it went!" My dad squats down beside me and rubs a sleeve between his fingers. His eyes take on a dreamy look. "Uncle Gus' sweater from the Montreal Canadiens. I wondered what became of it."

I hold up the sweater. How can this possibly be *that*?

"It can't be. Where is the famous C with the H inside? Besides it's way too small and it has holes."

"Well, it is." Grandpa chuckles. "In those days they didn't

wear as much equipment so it didn't have to be as large as today's. It's woollen, so it shrunk in the wash. And it's been washed quite a bit over the years. Uncle Gus gave it to me to use as a practice sweater — that's when the felt crest with the insignia fell off. Then all my kids wore it to play hockey in the backyard when they were little."

"Dad how could you?" I'm horrified at the disrespect shown the sacred object.

"We were kids. We didn't know any better."

I fold the sweater carefully. When the adults leave, I place it gently in the cedar chest.

* * *

Hotel Edouard VII
39 Avenue De L'Opera, Paris
Saturday, Dec. 15, 1934
Dear Spike,
...Each man looks after his own equipment and baggage. We have nice kit bags with a lock, for our hockey equipment, which consists of 2 pairs of skates, 2 sweaters and socks, 3 pucks each, about 5 lbs. of tape, on top of our playing outfit, and it's easily carried....

Joe

I lug my hockey bag into the dressing room. It's wall-to-wall bodies.

"Hey, Puff, over here." Kris, a boy from my school, waves to me.

I breathe a sigh of relief. It's good to see a familiar face even though we've never had much to do with each other except for a group project or two at school. He's a super jock while up till now I've just hacked around for fun when I've played a sport — nothing in common. To make room for me, he scrunches closer to Bart, one of his school buddies.

We help each other into our equipment. There seems to be a never-ending stream of it. I wriggle into the cup and garter belt. It feels incredibly uncomfortable. No one else seems to be bothered by this piece of gear. Embarrassed, I quickly slip on the pants — they're Dad's old ones. I attach the Velcro straps of the shin pads, pull a pair of socks over them and try to fasten the garters.

"Just drop the pants. It easier to do up the tabs before you put them on." Kris laughs.

I thought I was blushing already, but my face is flushing warmer. I stop struggling to reach up the pant leg and do as suggested. But I do it fast. I hate being in my underwear in front of strangers. I shrug into Dad's old shoulder pads and press the fasteners together. The elbow pads are next. From the hockey bag I pull out a blue and gold sweater. It's the Buffalo Sabres' uniform from the 1980s. Dad was a Sabres' fan.

I pull the sweater over my head. The back gets stuck on the shoulder pads.

"Here, let me help." Bart reaches over and pulls it down.

"Thanks." I take out my skates.

"Hey, guys, get a load of these. Gordie Howe signed! Are they for real?" Bart's grey eyes look as large as pucks.

"Na. They're just a special model, that's all."

"Same difference. Awesome." Kris strokes the signature with his big hands.

A tall thin man with a clipboard pokes his head into the room. "Everybody out on the rink."

I tug on my laces one last time and tie up my skates. They feel good.

As I head out of the dressing room, I see my reflection in

the glass panels and smile. Who is this dirty-blond, green-eyed hulk? I look huge. The Uncles never looked like this. Their protective gear wasn't as bulky and they didn't wear helmets. I jam mine onto my head. Bet they never waddled like a knight in armour either. I do.

Most of the kids on the ice are moving in a large circle like at Sunday free skating. Half a dozen or so are going against the flow. I see Ryan Thunderchild among them. Show-offs.

A whistle blows. In the centre of the ice stand three middle-aged men holding clipboards.

"Okay. Listen up. I want you guys at that end," the short bald one yells. "I want ten kids at a time to skate to the other end when I blow the whistle. First ten skaters line up. Quickly."

I hang back. Ten of the most macho guys challenge the other boys for the spots. The whistle blows and they streak down the ice. The next line forms. Ryan is with them. At the signal they dash toward the other end. This line wavers and disintegrates. The better skaters like Ryan reach the end while some are still struggling at centre. Reassured, I join the next group. When the whistle blows, I take off. Head down, I pump my legs as fast as I can. At the red line I glance up and see that our row has fallen apart. There's a big group in front of me. I thought I was flying. I look to each side but there's no one there. I peek over my shoulders and my heart drops — I'm bringing up the rear. That's okay, maybe I don't have to be fast. Mom says I'm the slow deliberate type. And Dad calls me methodical Joe — after Uncle Joe.

It's just my first year. I'll get better.

Ryan sidles up to me.

"Get lost," I say.

His eyes start to smoulder and he jabs me in the ribs with his elbows. Hard. "Puff, those ancestors must be puking."

My confidence sags.

When the last group makes it up the ice, the bald man blows the whistle to get our attention.

"Line up along the length of the rink. We'll practise stops and starts."

The whistle blows. We skate. It blows again. We stop. And so it goes — again, and again and again. I'm better at this. All the skating on Dad's little backyard rink has paid off.

The adults set up orange pylons. We try and stickhandle around them. I'm slow but accurate and my turns are good. Some of the speeders are bouncing off the cones and sending them flying. Ryan has hit every one. I love it.

At the end of the practice the thin man reads out a list of names. Mine is on it. He asks us to wait and dismisses the others. Kris, Bart and Ryan disappear in the direction of the dressing rooms.

I wait expectantly. The bald man waits until all but those on the list have left.

"Okay. I don't know if you kids are aware that these practices are tryouts for the A-level teams. Frankly you're not going to make it. But don't worry, you will be placed on house league teams. I suggest you stay home until your coaches give you a call." He skates off.

Hey, no big deal. That's all I wanted in the first place.

2

Welcome to the Dream

WINNIPEG FREE PRESS
Saturday, March 5, 1949
FORMIDABLE ARRAY OF PUCKSTERS CHOSEN ON JUVE-
NILE DREAM TEAM
...Romeo Rivers: The top coach in the league has a brilliant hockey history, having represented Canada at the 1932 Olympics as a member of the old Winnipegs. He toured Europe in 1935, being on the Canadian team which won the European crown that year. Mr. Rivers' coaching career consists mainly of three years with the West End Memorials, and two years with the Orioles...

January 27, 1930
Dear Stan,
Just getting my land legs after the long ride from Winnipeg. Would have liked to take a cab to the hotel and get some shut-eye before the game that night with Boston, but was picked up at the station by Hart's man and driven strait to the Montreal Forum for practice. The boys must have thought I was a real country bumpkin, I swear I was slack-jawed suiting up with the likes of Morenz and Joliat.

Tell Mama I'm fine. I wrote her already, but you know how

*she worries. Would you believe she stuck some dough in my
pocket as I got on the train...*

Gus

The dressing room is crowded. It's the first practice and a
parents' meeting, too. As I search for an empty spot, I see
familiar faces — kids from school. We wave to each other. I
find a place on the bench near the door, drop my hockey bag,
unzip it and start suiting up. Dad leans up against the small
piece of wall near the entrance.

"Hi there. Remember me?" the boy changing beside me
squeaks. "Scott."

It's the kid from the community club sign-ups.

"Yeah." I nod at him.

"You go to Darwin School don't you? The kids haven't
been the friendliest there." He brushes a lock of white-blond
hair off his forehead.

Is he hinting at me? I feel guilty that I had ignored him.

"I haven't seen you at school. You're not in my homeroom,"
I say in my defense.

"No. I'm in Mr. Kellet's. Are the kids in your room nicer?"

Relieved, I nod my head again. Ryan and a few other jerks
are in Kellet's class this year — not in mine, thank goodness.

"I saw you a couple of times. I waved but you didn't
notice."

"The halls are always crowded," I mumble guiltily.

"Yeah. And I'm kind of short." He laughs, letting me off the
hook.

No kidding, I think. His laugh is infectious and I can't help
smiling back. "I'll look for you at recess."

A couple of guys in their twenties walk in. One is slim with
dyed-blond spiky hair. The other is shorter, all muscle and has

a pierced ear. They look like they belong on stage not in a hockey rink.

Ryan Thunderchild follows them in. He shoulders his way to an empty spot and shrugs out of his jacket. Pulling off his tuque, he straightens his raven black mop. He dons his equipment ignoring those around him.

"Hope he's not their helper," I whisper to Scott.

"Probably just a player," Scott replies.

"Doubt it. He was quite good at the tryouts."

"You went to them? I didn't go. Knew I wouldn't make it."

"My friends said that's how they put you on teams. I thought I had to go. You see, it's my first time playing."

"No kidding. Mine too."

Blondie clears his throat to get our attention. "Hi there. I'm Rob Eastman. I'll be coaching this —"

"You look kind of young. How old are you anyway?" one of the parents interrupts.

"Old enough. Twenty-two if you must know." The coach stands up straight. His green eyes glint with defiance.

"I don't think that's important," Dad says.

"Yes it is. What kind of experience could he have?" The parent insists.

"Let the poor man speak. Maybe he'll tell us what we need to know," my father says.

A number of parents side with Dad.

"Yeah. Let him speak."

"Thanks." The coach nods at his defenders. "Like I was going to say. I've played hockey since I was five. Played junior hockey with the Fort Garry Blues. And I've got my level-one coaching certification. At present I'm taking a recreational sports course at the community college. Satisfied?" He glares at the complainer.

The man nods.

"I realize we have a mixed bag of talent here. Some of the kids have never even played before. My goals for this year are simple. I would like the kids to improve their skills. Learn some new ones. Develop an appreciation for the game. I don't think we can ask for much more."

There's a murmur of agreement from the parents.

The coach continues, "I would like to concentrate on the team and Mr. Hartford, here, has offered to be manager. I'm going to take him up on the offer." He points to a parent.

The man towers over the other dads. He smiles and waves acknowledgement. "Please call me Doug. I'm sure we all agree Rob should be allowed to focus on coaching. I'll be happy to act as a go-between. I'm sure if you have any concerns, I'll have them too because my son, Mick, is on the team." He points to a kid I don't know. The boy is cocky looking with blond-tipped brown hair. "I'm betting there won't be any problems because we all want the same thing — a winning season. I'll turn it back to Rob." He seems pleasant enough.

"Thanks. I'd like to introduce you to Brent Jenkins." He points at stubble head with the pierced ear. "He's my assistant coach. And for those who need to know," he says, scowling in the direction of the parent who complained, "Brent is twenty. Has played hockey for years. He's working on his level-one coaching and is taking the same college course as me. Okay?" No one raises an objection so he continues. "For the next two weeks we'll be practising Mondays, Wednesdays, and Thursdays. Seven till eight at the club. Be suited up and on the ice on time. Once the season starts we will be cutting back to just Mondays and Wednesdays. Game schedules aren't out yet. We'll get them to you as soon as they are. Any questions…? No…? The parents are free to go. We'll be out on the ice shortly."

When the door shuts behind the last parent Coach Eastman peaks again.

"We know why we're here. We want a piece of the Canadian dream. Every boy's goal is to play in the NHL. Saturday night is our special night. Without Hockey Night in Canada would we be Canadian? Even the immigrant understands that." He pauses, eyeing the kids in the room. Every so often his gaze lingers on a boy before moving on.

"Why's he looking at me?" whispers Sean Chan, a boy from my class. "My ancestors were building the railroad when Cory Brown's were still sipping tea in England."

"Here is where it all starts. In the community clubs across the country. On the rinks," the coach continued. "Welcome to Canada's game. Welcome to the dream. AND WHAT IS IT WE WANT?" He waits for a response.

The silence drags on too long.

"To be Canadian?" Ashok Prasad asks tentatively. He came from India to our school last year.

The coach ignores him and yells again "WHAT DO WE WANT?"

"What a crock this is," Scott whispers.

I don't say anything because I want a part of that dream.

There are murmurs from some of the boys.

"To play hockey?"

"To have fun?"

"To get exercise?"

"WHAT DO WE WANT?" An edge of irritation tinges his voice.

"To be a part of a tea —"

"TO BE A TEAM," Ryan cuts the boy off.

"RIGHT ON." Eastman punches the air above him. "What did he say?"

"TO BE A TEAM," we yell back.

"YEAH! HOO-HOO-HOO." Fist raised, he twirls his fore-arm at his elbow.

The assistant coach copies him. Soon a number of the boys have joined in. The whole thing has the feel of those live rock concerts they broadcast on the music channels.

I hesitate, then join in too.

Coach Eastman is beaming. "Okay, let's do it. Let's go build a team. To the rink."

"Rink number two." The assistant coach waves us in the right direction.

The air has the November nip to it — just cold enough to form good outdoor ice. Some of the parents who have stuck around, follow and lean on the boards watching.

"All right team. Do a couple laps to warm up." Eastman takes off around the rink.

I follow in what I now think of as my slow steady stride. This time however, I'm not the slowest. There are skaters strug-gling behind me. Scott wobbles up to me and we continue side by side.

"I'm liking this very much," Ashok calls back as he passes us, a grin flashing behind his mask. It's amazing how fast he's moving, skating like that, tipped over on his ankles.

Scott and I laugh, drawn in by his pure joy.

We're halfway around the rink when Ryan, Sean and Mick lap us. They're all big and fast. Actually the whole team is on the taller side of average. Scott and Ashok are the exceptions. Funny though, with their equipment on, they seem average while we look hulking.

A whistle sounds.

The coach motions us in. "Let's do some stretches."

On the ice the rock star image disappears. He's all jock.

We bend side to side. Do lunges. Sit on the ice and reach forward. Reach to the sides.

"Okay, back on your feet. Let's do some sculling," the coach yells.

Ryan, Sean and Mick, the three musketeers, take off. So do a few others. The rest of us stare blankly at Eastman.

"Sculling? Flat-footed skating? Okay. Place your heels together. Toes pointed out to the sides. Bend your knees. Form a diamond-shaped space between your legs. Push with your heels. Then quickly go in with your toes." He demonstrates as he speaks.

"Ooh. Makes little diamonds on the ice with your skates, too." Ashok tries to copy the coach. His feet get away on him and he sits down hard on the ice — his legs spread wide.

The team busts a gut. But it's not so funny when we try it. Some of us lucky ones don't fall, but our progress up the rink is painfully slow. And, we are the ones being laughed at by the three amigos as they glide past.

The coach blows the whistle again. "Looks like I'm going to have to work on the basics with some of you. Brent why don't you take those kids and work on their backwards skating?" He points at the better players. "Now the rest of you form a ring around the faceoff circle. We're working on balance. Okay, place your sticks inside the circle pointing at the dot. Feet shoulder-width apart. Bend your knees."

We lean one way, then the other. Bend our ankles in. Bend them out. Jump on two feet. Hop on one. Over and over again. Finally the coach blows the whistle.

"Once around the rink and then to the dressing room," he yells.

I waddle off the ice in the middle of the pack and pull off my helmet to soak in the cool refreshing air. I love early winter when the first snows blanket the drab land, trapping pollen and molds under it, freeing me from my asthma for a while.

"Well, sport? How was it?" Dad chucks my bag into the back of the van.

"All right, I guess." I'm not sure what else to say.

"You don't sound enthusiastic."

"I thought there would be more skating and less standing in a circle."

"The coach was working on basics. I'm sure it will get more exciting next time. Seems like an okay guy, too. He's got a lot of high-level playing experience for a community club coach." Dad pulls out of the parking lot.

"Uh-ha. But he gave us this corny spiel — to be Canadian is to play hockey. And then there was some rah-rah stuff."

"Team-building material? Hum. They do that in the adult world, too, bud. Supposed to help people work together."

"I think he got that from the course he's taking."

"Wouldn't be surprised. He's got a hard job ahead of him making such a motley crew into a team."

"What do you mean by that?" I snap at him.

"Ooo. Team loyalty. The team building must be working already. The skill levels range all the way from finesse skaters to ankle-draggers. That's all I mean, Lee. Nothing to take offense to." He turns into the driveway.

I lug my bag to the basement and hang up my things to air. He's right. Unfortunately, I'm closer to the ankle-draggers than the masters. To be the next great Rivers isn't going to be easy.

* * *

Whenever we hit the ice, Eastman makes us do the same routine as the first practices. Two laps, stretching and then into the two groups. We do the circle thing again. I'm about as sick of it as I can get. Finally, he changes drills.

This is more like it. I glide on one foot. We're still working on our balance. But at least we're moving.

"Race you," Ashok calls to Scott and me.

"You're on." I push off as hard as I can.

It's not much of a race. After the initial move, you're stuck with the speed you've got. I win anyway.

Scott brings up the rear. "Ashok you amaze me. How do you move so fast with your ankles bent?"

He shrugs. "You could say, I'm having great inside edges." His white teeth flash against his cocoa skin as he smiles.

I really like the guy — always happy and positive.

We keep racing through the sculling drills. The three of us are much better at this now.

"Way to go, guys. I swear the team is twice as fast as last time," Coach Jenkins yells.

We're not divided into two groups now. Pylons are set up and we practise stickhandling.

"Okay, time for some fun," Coach Eastman booms over the clatter of sticks on pucks and skates on ice. "British bulldog. And I'm *it*. You kids have to skate from one end of the rink to the other, back and forth. If I tag you between the blue lines, you have to join me and help tag the others. Now GO!"

I take off like a slapshot. On my third trip one of the ankle-draggers comes after me. I pump my legs faster — just make it over the line as he grabs my sweater.

"Safe."

He wobbles away after someone else.

The area between the blue lines is getting dangerous as more and more kids are tagged. As I make a dash for it, Ashok gives chase. I'm barely two strides ahead of him when I sidestep, pivot and head in the other direction. He reaches out to swat me. Windmills. Lets out a WO...OAH as his momentum takes him away from me.

"See ya," I taunt over my shoulders. I turn back to continue my dash only to find Scott smack dab in front of me. We collide and go down.

"Are you an *it*?" he squeaks.

I shake my head. We both scramble to our feet and take off in opposite directions, laughing.

Next trip I'm not so lucky. I'm tagged just as I cross centre. Scott's making a break for safety so I give chase. I grab his arm just as Coach Eastman's whistle blows.

"Okay, head for the change room. I'll be handing out sweaters and game schedules as you change."

Sweaters. Numbers. Two, eight, ten or sixteen. I can't decide which one I want — but it has to be one of those, they are The Uncles'.

We aren't given a choice. I touch my Gretzky skates for luck. The coach tosses a blue and red sweater at me. Number two. YES.

"Listen up. Make sure you give the schedules to your parents. We've only got three practices left before our first game. There's still a lot to work on, but the last one we'll scrimmage, to get the feel of a game."

3

Play Hockey and You're In

THE WINNIPEG EVENING TRIBUNE
Saturday, March 29,1930
*...Gustave Desriviers, better known as George Rivers to his
Winnipeg friends, brought the crowd to its feet by scoring the
goal that broke up the contest.*

February 3, 1930
Dear Stan,
*Extra! Extra! Read all about it. Get a load of these news clip-
pings. Hart's got the town believing that I'm of French
extraction. What a shock they'll get if they try and Parlez-vous
Français with me because the only French in me are the fries I
ate for lunch. HA. HA. But really, I have so many names now it
sure is crazy.*

Gustave Augustus George Spike (Gus)

I don't know what it is about guys and hockey, but once you're
on a team you are given more respect from the others who
play the sport. For years, like all the other boys who didn't play
organized hockey, I faced the subtle attitude of superiority from
the hockey jocks all winter long. This year it's not there. I'm
seen as one of them.

At afternoon recess, as usual, I join one of the groups forming a soccer game. I figure a good way to beat the cold is by running. As I strike out across the playground, I hear someone calling my name. Kris and Bart are waving at me from near the school doorway. I head back, wondering what he could want.

"So, how's the hockey going, rookie?"

"Okay,I guess," I hesitate, then I open up when he gives me the thumbs-up. "The last practice was so much fun. Our coaches are great, all they want is for us to improve."

"Good, good. Too bad they won't allow hockey sticks at school. It would beat freezing our butts off every recess."

"We could join one of the soccer games," I suggest.

"Na, soccer's a summer game. I like to focus on hockey during the winter. Bart and I are setting up a street-hockey game after school. Are you interested?"

"Sure," I say.

Scott waves from across the playground. He and Ashok are strolling together.

"Who's that with Ashok Prasad?" Bart elbows me.

"Scott Kessle. He's in Kellet's class."

"So how do you and Ashok know the wimp anyway?" asks Kris.

"We're on the same hockey team."

"That for real? Prasad's playing, too?" A disbelieving frown spreads across Kris' freckled face.

I nod, then brush back the lock of hair that falls into my eyes.

"Do you think they'd like to play road hockey with us, too? Hey, Prasad. Over here," Bart yells across the field.

Like I said — play hockey and you're in.

As they reach us, Ryan comes flying around the corner and bumps Scott. The smaller boy stumbles into Kris.

"Watch where you're going, loser." Kris stares daggers at the loner. They stand glued at the nose for a moment. "Get lost, Thunderchild."

Ryan breaks eye contact and saunters off.

"Jerk. Can't even look a man in the eye," Kris sneers.

"Wonder what team he's playing for? Thought he'd be on ours. Must have made Double A." Bart ran his hand through his chestnut curls.

"He's playing with us," I say.

"You're kidding. I wonder why? He's good."

"Sean Chan's on our team, too. We're not all crappy players." It irritates me that they assume our team is all castoffs.

"That, I understand. There are too many tournaments at the A-levels. His life's too busy with his music."

The buzzer rings and we head for class.

* * *

"WHO ARE WE?" The coach is standing with his arm stretched above his head, his hand a fist.

"THE JOHN FORSYTH JETS," we yell back on cue.

"AND WHAT DO WE DO?"

"PLAY HARD."

"AND WHAT DO WE WANT?"

"TO CREAM THE BRUINS."

"YEAH. HOO-HOO-HOO." He does the arm-twirling thing again. We join in.

"TO THE RINK."

We follow the coach to our bench. I glance at the spectators. I'm surprised that there are so many fans on a Thursday night. My grandpa and dad are up there in the stands. There are three generations of Rivers in the building, maybe more, because I feel as if Romie, Joe and Gus are up there to cheer me on in my first game, also.

"Listen up." Eastman raps the boards with a stick. "Two laps and stretches. Then warm up the goalie."

I skate across the rink, soaking in the feel of the ice beneath my feet. The sounds in the arena sing to me — the snick of the blades on the ice, smack of stick on puck and twack of the puck on boards. Same ones The Uncles must have heard. I love them all.

The whistle shrills and I head for the bench. My stomach is a tight knot. Were they ever this nervous? During the World Cup or any other playoffs?

On the ice Ryan is taking the faceoff. Scott is to his left. I give him the best thumbs-up I can manage with the thick gloves on. He waves back.

The ref drops the puck and Ryan gets control. He twirls and takes off down the ice, an opponent hot on his tail. The Glenwood Bruins' defense press, forcing him to pass. Scott has chased the play and Ryan lobs one right onto his stick. Scott takes a few strides but decides he can't make a move. He lifts his stick to whack the puck, loses his footing and lands flat on his tush. I realize he's been using the stick as a stabilizer. A black-jerseyed Bruin swoops and takes the puck down the ice. By the time the kid hits our blue line, Ryan is right there with him. Ryan knocks the puck off his stick. Our left defense nabs it and passes it up the ice — hard. It ricochets off the boards and into the stands. The lines change.

Sean takes his place in the faceoff circle. I skate to the left of him. Ashok grins at me from the other side. The puck falls and Sean digs at it. No luck. The Bruins' centre slaps it to his right wing. The boy picks it up, glides around me and is gone. I pump as fast as I can after him, but I just can't catch up to the play. Ashok is in hot pursuit of his man. He shuffle-runs with him, keeping himself between the two players — tying up his winger. Our defense makes for the boy with the puck and forces him to pass the rubber back. I intercept and take the play down the ice. Their right defenseman comes at me so I aim the puck for Ashok's stick. Bulls eye. Slow but accurate that's me. He fans on a pass and loses his footing. A Bruin picks up the puck and glides by. I give chase, but fall behind. With two of us out of the play, Glenwood gets a clear shot on net. Cory Brown, our goalie, sweeps at it, but, in it goes. Shift over, I head for the bench.

"Just great. I thought I signed up for hockey, not Clowns on Ice," Mick mumbles to Ryan. "Don't know why they stuck me on this joke of a team. Or you, either. We don't belong here." He shakes his head as he jumps onto the ice.

I ignore the comments and focus on the game.

Mick wins the faceoff and dipsy-doodles all over the ice. For a long while it looks like a game of tag not hockey.

I feel an elbow in my side.

"Mick Hartford, he is very good. But I'm thinking that he should be passing. That is the game, is it not?" Ashok asks.

I nod without taking my eyes off the action.

The black jerseys put two men on Mick and he finally coughs up the puck. The play moves to our end. There's a weak shot at the net. Cory falls on the puck and the ref blows the whistle. Scott's line moves onto the rink.

Ryan gets the puck to our winger on the faceoff. The boy tries to deke around a Bruin and gets bumped off the puck. Ryan sweeps the disk onto his stick and swerves around an opponent. Two more come at him — boxing him in. Scott is open and in front of the net. Ryan hesitates for a moment, then taps it to him. Scott lifts his stick to shoot and down he goes. The loose puck is snapped up by our other winger. He drills it back to Ryan who one-times it at the net. It slices through the five-hole — the space between the goalie's legs. Our team goes wild and we bang our sticks against the boards. Scott jumps at Ryan to hug him and they both topple. I laugh and look up into the stands. Dad and Grandpa are clapping and cheering. If The Uncles could see this, I know they would be cheering, too. There is nothing as wonderful as the team's first goal.

Each shift seems an eternity as I wait to get on the ice. And then, my shift passes in the blink of an eye. The butterflies are gone. Even though the score is four to one for Glenwood when the final whistle blows, I feel great. This is my sport.

As I pass, Grandpa winks and says, "Good game, Lee."

In the dressing room the coaches are all smiles.

"Way to go, guys!" Assistant Coach Jenkins high-fives the kid next to him. "There's no shame in losing when you've played your hearts out. And all you kids did just that."

"Big deal," Mick Hartford mumbles. He strips off his gloves and chucks them violently into his hockey bag.

"Cheer up. It's not that bad." Coach Eastman puts his arm around Mick's shoulder. "The good thing about losing the first game is you have nowhere to go but up. Right? We'll do better next time."

Mick shrugs off the coach's arm and continues to take out his disappointment on his equipment as he changes.

As Ryan is leaving he stops in front of me.

"What do *you* want?" I challenge him.

"Oh, nothing." He moves away two steps then turns back to me scowling. "You must have descended from the runt of the Rivers' litter, eh, Lee? You've got none of the talent that your uncles had."

* * *

I love Friday nights. The whole weekend stretching before me. No need to do homework right away. If I were alone, I'd turn off the white lights that are strung up in the trees that edge the rink and I'd lie on the ice staring up at the stars. But I'm not alone — Scott, Ashok, Kris and Bart are on my rink playing one-on-one. I figured I should invite them after they invited me to play street hockey.

"...so I poke checked the puck." Kris makes like he's living it. "I scooped it up. And stickhandled to the blue line. Aimed for the corner." He takes a shot at the empty net. "And bingo. Just like that. What a beaut." He raises his arms and does a victory dance.

"Yup, that was some game," Bart sighs. He sweeps the puck out of the net. "How'd you guys do?"

For a moment I'm back at the arena, chasing the puck just like The Uncles. "It was awesome."

"Whipped their butt? Right on." Kris extends his mittened palm for five.

I blush, ignoring his hand. "Well... no...four to one."

"Nothing wrong with that. Put it there pal." He waves his hand at me.

"For them, you dork." Ashok giggles.

"Huh? But you said awesome." Bart looks at me with disbelief.

"It was. The skating, the action, the whole team thing. Oh, never mind..." I can see he's not getting it. I pick up the puck and move to the end of the rink. Ashok takes his place in front of the goal. Skating down the ice, I fake a right, glide around to the left and shoot. The puck dings off the crossbar and into the bank of snow that edges the rink.

"That explains why Thunderchild growled at me when I asked how the game went," Kris says.

"Yeah, right. Like the way you asked, wasn't reason enough? 'Hey, Cryin' Blunderchild did you win?'" Bart mimics Kris.

"Well he's not the sharpest knife in the draw — is he?"

Ashok's smile slides off his face and his dark eyes dim.

"Prasad, I was just joking and he knew it. He has no sense of humour. Does Rivers get ticked when I call him Puff?"

I'd like to tell him that it bugs me, but that would be a waste of breath. These last couple weeks I've found out that Kris is always right, or so he thinks. I regret getting chummy with him — he's so full of himself. I think I'm going to avoid him from now on.

"That's different, everyone calls him Puff," Bart answers. "Anyway, speaking about Thunderchild, I know why he is not playing A-level."

"No kidding. Okay, Bart old pal, share." Kris puts his arm around Bart's shoulders.

We gather around not wanting to miss a word.

"Our coach said he cut him because his father is a pushy, interferring so-n-so."

"What're you trying to pull? The coach never told us nothing, or has he suddenly become buddy-buddy with you?"

"Course not. I was with my dad when we bumped into the coach at the store. And you know how adults are, they start to talk and forget that there's a kid around. Well, my dad's the hockey convenor at the club, and from what I could figure out, there was a really pushy parent who caused all kinds of trouble last year. Even though his son should have made Triple A, every coach cut the kid from their roster. They didn't want any hassle from the dad."

"Are you sure it's Ryan they were talking about? His dad seems as quiet as he is," Scott says.

"It's got to be. Who else at the tryouts was that good and isn't playing A-levels?"

"You're right," Kris said, nodding. "There were a lot of good players, but the only awesome kid I remember is Ryan."

I still have my doubts. No way can I see Mr. Thunderchild being pushy. I dig the puck out of the snow, toss it to Scott and glide to the net.

4

The Three Amigos

WINNIPEG EVENING TRIBUNE
Thursday, January 23,1930
*...The break which sent the Monarchs on the way to victory came
after.... Gentleman Joe Rivers, the elongated regal defenseman,
carried the puck into Falcon territory and slipped a pass to his
brother Romeo, whizzing down left wing. Cutting in with added
speed Romeo fired and his high-burning drive left Bud Simpson
helpless...*

March 20,1930
Dear Stan,
*I got my first NHL goal in the game against the New York Amer-
icans last night. Late in the third I nabbed a pass from Morenz
at the opponents' blue line and made a rush for the goal. A flick
of the wrist and in it went. The Americans are plenty rugged and
at first I was intimidated, but once I got my goal I was so excited that the next thing I knew I was hauling down their winger
and cooling my heels in the penalty box. What a swell night. I
truly feel like one of the pros now...*

Gus

I can't believe I'm sitting in my underwear with a bunch of other guys and not blushing beet red. All the parents have wandered out of the dressing room while we change for practice. I adjust my knee pads, pull the socks over them and do up the garter.

The assistant coach clears his throat. "Excellent game, guys. For a team with so many novices, you did one heck of a job."

Coach Eastman nods. "But, having said that, some of you need a lot more work on basic skills to be effective on the ice. We've decided to stick with the old groups. Brent will be working with the weaker players. For the first half of each practice we'll concentrate on developing individual skills. The second half we'll regroup and focus on teamwork. Any questions?"

"Yeah, any chance of us getting off this team of bozos?" Mick puts his arms over Ryan's and Sean's shoulders.

The assistant coach glares at them. "We expect better sportsmanship from our more experienced players."

"Hey, no problem here." Sean's almond eyes blink nervously as he removes Mick's arm from his shoulders. "I chose to play at this level."

Ryan shrugs out from the embrace and silently ties up his skates.

Coach Eastman ignores Mick's comment and continues, "No questions? All right." He raises his fist. "WHO ARE WE?"

"THE JETS," we yell back.

"AND WHAT DO WE WANT?"

"TO BE A TEAM."

"RIGHT ON." Brent Jenkins twirls his arm at the elbow. "HOO, HOO, HOO"

The team joins in.

"To the rink," the coach calls out, pointing to the door.

We're back doing sculling, one-foot skating, hopping and

jumping but Coach Jenkins tries to make it fun. We do relays, play redlight-greenlight and tag.

We scrimmage for the second half of the practice. Ashok and I are on the same line. Sean is our centre. He faces off against Ryan and loses the puck. Ryan takes it up the ice a bit then drops it back to Mick, who flies by me as I try to follow. He glances over his shoulder, sees I've fallen behind and returns.

"Come and get it," he taunts, stickhandling around me.

I make a stab at the puck.

"Oow. Look at the fight...er. Come on sucker." He leaves the puck unguarded for a second and I go for it again. With lightning reflexes, he sweeps up the puck and turns to leave. Sean is right there. He knocks Mick off the puck. Ashok picks it up but Ryan strips it off him, skates to the net and scores. Sean and our defense try to keep us in the game but Mick and Ryan skate circles around us — mocking our lack of skill.

"Whatever made those jokers think they could play hockey, eh Ryan?" Mick laughs and pats Ryan on the back.

By the time the practice is over I'm pooped. I'm moving in slow mo, like after an asthma attack, so I'm the last to finish changing. Mr. Hartford and the coaches are chatting in the doorway. Their backs are to me so they don't see me standing there wanting out. I wait for a break in the conversation to excuse myself, trying not to eavesdrop, but it's impossible.

"Yeah... I agree they did okay. But there's so many weak players," Mr. Hartford complains.

"Give them time, they'll improve," the assistant coach says.

"Sure, sure. But you've got to admit we're weak on offense. We don't even have one line with two strong forwards. With another strong winger we'd stand a chance."

"You're right. We could use some power up front, but we've

got what we've got." Jenkins shrugs.

"Hold on there, Brent, it's not like the lines are etched in stone," Coach Eastman chuckles. "Why don't we put two stronger players together next game? What have we got to lose?"

There's no lull in the conversation, so, I tap Jenkins on the shoulder. I can't hang around any longer, Dad's waiting.

* * *

Game two and my heart's thumping. Every evening I've been practising the drills Coach Jenkins did with us. To follow in The Uncles' footsteps is going to be hard work. The first game made it obvious that I've got a long way to go just to be average.

The coaches have rearranged the lines, like I heard them say they would. Ryan and Mick are the power twosome that are going to start the game. Ashok, Scott and I have been placed on the same line. ALL RIGHT.

The puck drops and Mick knocks it to Ryan. He twirls around the Norberry Royals' forward and is gone. Mick's right up there with him to receive the pass. He dekes around the winger checking him, then dipsy-doodles around their centre. He's heading for the net when the puck is stripped off his stick. A Royal retrieves it and takes the play out of their zone. Our right-winger cuts the guy off, forcing him to pass. Mick intercepts and heads the play in the other direction — a red and blue streak weaving among the white sweaters of the Royals. He stickhandles around three opponents before they stop him and move the action toward our end. The skater is checked off the puck and it slides over our blue line. Our defenseman clears it to Ryan, who makes a sweet pass to Mick. He swerves around one forward then pivots around their centre. Norberry double-teams him. Our right-winger bangs his stick on the ice to signal he's open. Mick ignores him, tries to go through both the skaters who are boxing him in and coughs up the puck again. The Royals make a two-line pass, so the whistle blows.

This is what I've been waiting for. Coach Eastman has me at centre with Ashok on my right and Scott on the left. When the puck drops I take a jab at it, but their centre grabs possession. He goes around me like I'm a pylon. Scott and Ashok are already chasing the play. I pivot and follow. By the time I pass Scott at the blue line, Ashok has his player tied up. I know I can't catch the centre, so I try to take out the other winger. I leave our defense to take care of the man with the puck. They pinch him in. He makes a wild pass, the puck slides across the ice, ending harmlessly along the boards. Scott wobbles over to grab it and dribbles a weak pass onto my stick. I take the puck up ice a bit, then whack it over to Ashok. A white jersey picks it off before it gets to Ashok and cranks one to his winger. The whistle shrills. Offside.

Sean's line does better than we did. They get the play down to the Royals' zone and even get a shot on net before their shift ends.

The hotshots are back on. Ryan flies down the ice. Our wingers are with him. It's a three-on-two — our forwards against their defense. Our right forward takes out one of Norberry's defenders. The other presses Ryan. Ryan fakes to the right but dekes left. On the fly, he passes to Mick, who one-times it right into the net. Mick is doing his victory dance when the buzzer goes. There's hooting, hollering and a whole lot of noise from our bench. Coach Eastman high-fives the guys as they come off.

By my first shift of the second period I'm still high from our one-goal lead. The adrenaline's pumping and I actually win the faceoff. Ashok receives the pass and takes off in that shuffle-run gait of his. He leaves the man checking him behind, only to run into the Royals' centre. The puck is stolen off his stick and the skater brings it all the way to our zone. He takes a shot. Our defense sweeps the puck off to the side. Crud, a white sweater is there to pounce on it and whack, it's in our net.

As we step off the ice, the coaches tap us on the helmets saying, "Don't sweat it; there's lots of time."

Mick thinks differently. "Just like in the movies, the jokers foul things up and get the audience laughing at them; then the heroes — that's you and me — come in and clean up the mess. Right partner?" He extends his palm to Ryan. Ryan hesitates for a moment before giving him five.

When the third period begins we're down by two. Ryan and Mick go into high gear. They keep the play in Norberry's end for their whole shift and finally pop one in. They do the same on their second shift.

"Rivers. Don't screw up. Think about those famous uncles," Ryan whispers, grabbing me as I pass to get on the ice.

I rip my arm out of his grasp and go to the faceoff circle. I work my butt off the whole shift. Our whole line does and it pays off. We don't get out of our end, but we don't get scored on either.

There's only two minutes left in the game and I'm relieved. Oh, I know there's plenty of time for the Royals to score — but if they do, it won't be my fault.

Sean wins the faceoff. He takes the play up to the opponent's blue line then passes to our winger. The kid has nowhere to go so he passes back to Sean. He moves the puck a few more feet before it's stolen off his stick. The player takes it all the way into our end. Our defensemen press — forcing him behind the net. Sean checks him from the other side. They wind up fighting for the puck along the boards until the buzzer goes.

As we collect our stuff to go to the dressing room, Mr. Hartford leans over the glass on our bench. "Way to go, guys!" He turns to the coaches. "What did I tell you? All they needed was a little more power up front."

"Looking good, Lee. Nice faceoff in the second." Dad extends his palm to me. "Put it there, buddy." I high-five him.

* * *

The way I figure it, after last game's win, the coaches will keep the dynamic duo on the same line from now on. So I'm not surprised when Coach Eastman calls out the starting lineup.

"Ryan Thunderchild, centre. Mick Hartford, left wing. Bob Paquet, right wing — "

"He's not coming. He's sick," someone calls out.

"Darn. We're short a winger then." The coach sighs. "Okay, we'll have to rotate you forwards through the lines." He glances at the roster and says, "Lee Rivers go on with Ryan and Mick first shift."

Mick rolls his eyes.

"Hey, I'm as disappointed as you. I'd rather be with Scott and Ashok," I mumble.

I take my place on the rink across from a hulking yellow-sweatered Viking. Mick wins the faceoff and gets the puck to Ryan. They take off down the ice. Out of my league, I follow as best I can. They control the play. The only good thing is that the Glenlee Vikings have some weaker players. I attach myself to one of these and try to keep him out of the game. For the most part I'm successful.

Mick and Ryan pepper the goalie with shots. One dings off the crossbar, over the glass and into the crowd.

I go to the bench, relieved the shift's over.

The next time I'm on the ice it's with Scott, thank goodness. We're the wingers. I fit into this line. The ref drops the puck and the Vikings take it down the rink. Their centre gets to our blue line, stops, looks for the open man then zaps one to him. By this time I've caught up to the play and I block the winger's path. He tries to get around me and loses the puck in the process. Scott skates by, scoops it up and wobbles off along the boards. I get open and he taps it to me. Our centre is clear, waiting for my pass. Twack. It's right on his stick. He takes it over the red line. My heart starts to bang in my chest. I've made it out of our end zone for the first time without a hotshot on my line. But my excitement doesn't last long, the Vikings check us. Scott and I are left behind as the play moves back to our end. We watch helplessly as they pop one into the net.

The lines change again. The power duo are back on. And this time they have Sean with them. Mick wins the faceoff once more. He dekes around the player checking him. Goes past two more. At the Vikings' blue line, their defense are waiting for him. He tries to outmaneuver them but is checked off the puck. A yellow sweater picks it up and takes the puck around his net, finds his open man and lobs it over. Sean steals it before it gets there. He zings it to Ryan. Ryan can't make a move. He whacks it back. Sean finds Mick's stick and he drills it at the net. YES.

Sean throws himself at Ryan. Mick dances his victory dance. We bang our sticks on the boards with glee.

A few seconds later Mick is dancing again. The three musketeers have made the sweetest three-on-two and nabbed us another goal.

By the end of the third period the whole team's dancing. We've cleaned up — seven to two. The three amigos' line has put in every goal of ours but one. That was scored by Ryan when Scott and I were on the ice. It was a breakaway and Scott and I weren't even in the play.

As we come off the ice, Mr. Hartford is all over us — giving high-fives and pats on the back. He's as excited as if he played the game. "Rob, did you see that? They're awesome!"

The friendly giant keeps patting first one, then the other of the coaches on the back. They're beaming, too. Just watching them I feel my excitement balloon.

"Mick, Sean and Ryan — they were meant to play together. Please tell me you won't split them up."

I should have known he wasn't talking about the whole team. Oh, well.

"They *were* good together, weren't they?" Coach Eastman agrees.

"Well? Going to keep them together permanently, or not?" Hartford follows the team to the dressing room.

The three men stop just outside the door.

"I don't know, Rob. It just doesn't seem right. It's kind of like stacking the deck or something." Jenkins strokes his stubbled jaw.

"Don't be stupid, Jenkins. There's nothing in the rule books that says you have to spread your talent through the lines evenly."

"Maybe not, but you'd like to make sure the weaker players aren't taken out of the game because no one on the line is good enough to get the puck."

"Rob. Help me out here. A line like that comes along once in a lifetime. Who are we harming by letting them do the job they can?" The large man dwarfs Coach Eastman as he places his arm on the coach's shoulder.

"He's right, Brent. They play the puck like an atom's line of Lindros, LeClair and Renberg. You've got to admit it's exciting to watch. What do you say we see what they can do? We could always change back," the coach coaxes his friend.

Brent Jenkins rubs his shaved head then gives it a shake. "Fine." He steps into the dressing room and waits to close the door behind Coach Eastman.

5

Insult to Injury

THE WINNIPEG EVENING TRIBUNE
Saturday, March 29,1930
After nearly five periods of overtime...passed and the fans wondering just how much longer the teams would remain deadlocked, Gustave Desriviers, better known as George Rivers to his Winnipeg friends, brought the crowd to its feet by scoring the goal that broke up the contest.

April 1, 1930
Dear Stan,
I'm in the doghouse. No one will speak to me — the French guys because they can't and the English because they won't. I made the mistake of stripping the puck from Morenz in a scrimmage. How was I supposed to know it was a unwritten law you don't show up the stars? I was just flying after our win against the Rangers. That was one grueling game. By the fifth period of overtime, most of the team was dead on their feet. I might have been one of the few fresh legs left but my goal was a swell one all the same. The fans in the Forum went wild. They stormed the dressing room, hefted me on their shoulders and carried me through the streets. It would have been great except I was stripped down to my underwear when I was kidnapped...

Gus

Ryan limps into the dressing room after the practice. He drops to the bench and sits there, eyes closed, leaning against the wall. I'm the only one still in the room when he starts to change. I watch him take his skates off carefully. There is a dark stain on his gray woollen socks. He gingerly pulls it off. Peeling back the bandage, he inspects his foot. It isn't bleeding anymore but the wound is ugly and raw.

"Awe, crud!" he curses under his breath. Looking up, his chocolate eyes lock with mine. His turn cold. "What're you gawking at?"

I quickly look down and concentrate on packing my equipment.

Mr. Thunderchild walks in. "You're slow today, Ryan."

"Look." Ryan holds his foot out.

His dad lets out a low whistle. "Doesn't look good. Get dressed. We're getting that checked at the walk-in. How long has it been like that?"

Ryan glance my way and hesitates before answering. "Since last practice. There's a rivet sticking up from the bottom of my skate."

I know he wishes me gone, so I quickly stuff my skates in my bag and leave. In the hall I stop to do up the zipper. It won't pull closed unless I rearrange my gear.

"Maybe we can tap it down and tape a thin piece of foam over — " Mr. Thunderchild's gruff voice reaches me in the hall.

"Yeah, right. These skates are falling apart. This blade holder is cracked and superglued together. The tongue on that one is ripping off and is duct-taped. There's more patching than original skate. You know I need new ones."

"I know, pal. Maybe you can have them for Christmas."

"CHRISTMAS. That's weeks away."

"Ryan, with the holidays coming, the cash just isn't there for extras."

"Look at my foot. With all the skating I do, this isn't an extra."

My bag's packed and I know I should go wait for Dad in the front hall, but I don't move. I'm mesmerized by what I'm hearing.

"Unfortunately, when a family is just getting back on their feet, skates are an extra. The timing's bad."

"The timing's always been wrong since we moved to Winnipeg. Last year, you dragged us here after Christmas. And for what? Some stupid temporary job."

"I've got a steady job now..." Ryan father tries to explain but Ryan isn't listening.

"The kids tried to be friendly but they ask me to do stuff that costs money. How could I tell them I didn't have any? So, I said no, and they thought I was a jerk. It was the middle of the school year — exam time — I didn't have a clue about what they were doing so then they thought I was stupid, too. Then the teacher gave us this family history project. I told them about our ancestors and how Grandfather taught me to trap, hunt and fish. And these city kids asked how could I eat Bambi's mom? And now, whenever I try to talk to someone, they look like they're waiting for me to sucker-punch them."

I feel sick because I'm guilty on all counts.

He continues, "Then I get angry and say something stupid that makes things worse. It's hard to keep my nose clean, like you want me to, when the only kids who will hang with me are the troublemakers. I want to go back to The Pas."

"We can't do that, Ryan. We're settled here. I've got a good-paying job now and we can pay off our debts."

"*I'm* not settled here. And you had a good job at the mill.

They didn't lay you off. You quit! You quit — and dragged us down here."

"You know I couldn't stay after your uncle Johnny died. Every where I looked I was reminded of him. Images of the accident would then fill my head. The logs getting loose from the truck. Coming down on us, like an avalanche. Covering him. Pinning him under. The memories are awful."

"That's where you and I are different. I saw Johnny everywhere too. But the memories were all good. I saw us getting sodas at the café. Fishing at the lake. Going to watch the OCN Blizzards play hockey. The familiar places made me feel closer to him. I miss him a lot."

"Me too, Ryan." There is silence, then the sound of a back being patted. "Look, the best I can do is buy the skates as an early gift. There won't be anything under the tree for you on Christmas Day, though, and I'll hate that. But the choice is yours. Come, we better get moving."

I grab my bag and hightail it to the foyer.

* * *

It's a beautiful December afternoon — faded blue-jean skies and bright sun glinting off the snow. Scott, Ashok and I are hacking around on my rink again.

"So what do you want for Christmas?" Scott asks as he taps the puck to me from in front of the goal.

"All I want is a vintage replica Montreal Canadiens' jersey. Just like Uncle Gus'." I squint as I take a slapshot at the net.

"I wouldn't mind the new hockey video game. Have you seen the graphics?" Scott picks up the puck and lobs it to Ashok.

"Ashok, what's on your Christmas wish list?" I ask.

"I am not celebrating this day, Christmas. I am a Hindu."

"You mean no tree? No presents? No lights —"

"We have lights." Ashok eyes twinkle. "Divali, festival of lights, was in November. We put lights all over the house. We had sparklers, too. As beautiful as this." He waves at the hoar-frost on the trees.

"But no presents for Christmas?" Ashok shakes his head and I continue, "That sucks."

I think of the other kid who might not have anything under the tree and ask, "What would you do if you needed something really badly, but could only get it if you didn't get any Christmas presents?"

"For me it would not matter. But you are not having any presents for Christmas either?" Ashok misunderstands. "I am so sorry."

"No, no. Not me." I tell them about Ryan's choice: skates or a Christmas gift.

"That blows. Why would his parents do that to him?"

I hesitate. I know Ryan wouldn't want the world to know he's poor, but I also know I wouldn't want anyone to think my parents were mean. So I tell my friends everything I overheard.

"Huh, that's his story. He's in my room, you know. I always wondered why he hardly ever hangs around with anyone. Most kids keep their distance, so I do too. I've never given him a chance." Scott shakes his head.

"None of us really have. We probably gave up too easily."

"I was certainly worried when I came here two years ago, but most of the kids were kind. When I hesitated they figured it was because I came from where things are done differently. They did not give up on me. What I am thinking is, it would be good to be nicer to Ryan."

Scott and I nod in agreement.

* * *

The arena lights glint off Ryan's new skates. His patched hockey pants seem out of place since our sweaters and socks are fairly new. He takes four quick laps around the rink — flying faster than he ever has. Then he makes a perfect stop in front of the bench, spraying ice shavings. There's a ghost of a smile on his lips. He grabs his worn stick, nabs a puck and heads to warm up Cory. My own equipment may be mostly old, but it looks new. And I know Dad wouldn't have to hesitate a moment if I needed anything. My life is easy — there will be lots of presents under my tree.

I elbow Ashok and Scott and point to the skates.

"That means no presents," Scott whispers.

We stop stretching, reach for our sticks from the pile and join him.

"Looking good," I say as he slaps a shot past Cory.

He nods and grunts in reply. Ashok chases the puck that Cory has cleared and passes it to Ryan. He whacks it to me and I take a shot on goal. The whistle blows and we head for our bench.

We're playing the Greendell Falcons and the three amigos are our starting forwards. Mick wins the faceoff. His pass is captured by Sean, who barrels down the ice. At the blue line Sean whacks the puck to Ryan. Ryan banks it off the boards to Mick and he one-times it at the net. Twang. The puck dings off the post and falls in the corner by the boards. The Falcons' defenseman swoops on it, glides around the net and up the other side. He slides it to his winger. Sean intercepts the pass and the play is back up the rink. Ryan slaps the ice, the puck thunks on his stick and he directs it into the goal. YES. We change up lines for the next faceoff.

"Great goal." I tap Ryan's pads as he passes. The ghost smile flickers across his face and he nods.

I skate to the right of the faceoff circle. Scott takes his place on the left. Ashok is centre. He tries hard, but his opponent easily grabs the puck and is halfway to our blue line before we even move. The three of us skate as fast as we can to catch up to the play. Our defense steps up to challenge the puckhandler. He dumps it along the boards and I manage to pull it to me. Our end is a sea of green as all five of the Falcons are there. Their defense tie up ours. Two of their wingers close in on me, so I look to make a pass. Scott has lost his footing and is on his tush again. Ashok is shuffling back and forth, like a duck in a shooting gallery, trying to lose the man who is taking him out of the play. I'm forced to take it around my own net. A Falcon is waiting for me. He poke-checks the puck off my stick, dekes around our defense and lobs one at the net. Cory doesn't even see it coming and it dribbles between his legs. One all. He whacks the goalpost with his stick in disgust.

"Thank goodness the three stooges are finally off," Mick snickers and pokes Ryan in the ribs. A dark scowl spreads across Ryan's face.

Our third line is as weak as mine, but they manage to hold off the Falcons. We do too, on our next shift. The three amigos on the other hand, not only keep the play in the Falcons' end during theirs, but bag us another goal before the period ends.

"ALL RIGHT. Doing good. Keep it up boys." Coach Eastman is all smiles.

The second period is much the same as the first. Ryan's line keeps the play in the Falcons' zone while my line struggles to get the play out of ours. The green sweaters get a couple of great shots on net during my shifts. Cory covers up beautifully. No goals are scored by either team.

"Way to go, guys! Protecting the lead. Good defensive play." The coach is still smiling.

The whistle blows and I line up for the faceoff. The Falcons' centre captures the puck and drops it back for his winger to pick up. I give chase as he flies toward our blue line. Surprising myself, I catch up and actually force him to cough up the puck. I pick it up, twirl away from him and skate for centre. Hot on my tail, he knocks the puck off my stick. Ashok hurries toward it. He's beaten by the Greendell Falcons' centre, who whacks it back behind the blue line. Their winger beats our defenseman. Dekes around him. Shoots. The puck finds the right corner of the net and the score is two-all.

The third line plays hard and keeps Greendell from scoring even though the play stays in our end. When it's their turn, the three amigos turn up the pressure and pepper the Falcons' goalie. Arm and legs flying, the kid holds them off. He wilts to the ice like soggy lettuce as the shift change is called.

Ryan taps my helmet as we squeeze past each other to exchange places on the ice. "Rivers, think of those uncles."

He's said that kind of thing before, but this time I realize it's not a dig.

I'm determined not to let the Falcons score. Ashok and Scott seem to have the same idea. We keep icing the puck — whacking it all the way to the other end of the rink. It comes right back to our end but we keep it out of our net. The score stays unchanged until the last shift of the game. The three amigos dominate the play. Once again the Falcons' goalie is pelted with shots. This time two slip past him so when the buzzer goes our team hoots our four-to-two victory.

Mr. Hartford grabs Coach Eastman as he steps off the ice. "I think we've got our Legion of Doom line. We're going to be number one."

6

Celebrations

Park - Hotel Bernerhof, Basel
Saturday, February 9, 1935
Dear Gang,-
...I am writing now as "veltmeisterschoft" meaning here the
World's Champions, and it stands for something to the people of
Europe, although in Canada they laugh at it and take it for
granted that we win it. Here they consider it much bigger than
the Olympics at Lake Placid in 1932 as there were 15 nations
represented at Davos, and if we slipped the least little bit and
lost there would be a lot of howling back home...
That's all for the present.

Joe

April 9, 1930
Dear Stan,
Never thought I'd be writing you as a Stanley Cup Champion
my first year in the NHL. What a finish to the season! Romie
will be crowing that it was the lucky rabbit's foot he sent me that
did the trick. I'm sure Morenz and the boys would dispute that.
Hainsworth's shutout in the final game against Boston was
golden...

Gus

A shok is examining our tree.

All around us is seasonal stuff, even the mugs we are using have Santa, reindeer and angels on them. My mom decorates every room this time of year.

"It must be weird not celebrating Christmas."

He turns to me. "Why? Do you feel strange not celebrating Hanukkah?"

"No…but that's different. Christmas is everywhere you look. Don't you miss being a part of it?" Scott asks.

"I am a part of it — maybe not the church stuff. But I can enjoy the music, decorations and good food." He picks up a shortbread cookie and pops it into his mouth. "Anyway, Santa isn't religious, so my parents are thinking, maybe, this year he will come to our house, too. I am thinking, what fun."

Ashok's face is glowing like the lights on the tree. I love Christmas time and I want everyone to be happy. I am so glad that all my friends can have an exciting holiday.

I remember Ryan and picture Christmas morning in his house. Everyone opening presents except him. I can't let that happen.

"You know what I'm thinking," I say. "I'm thinking, Ryan's house is going to get an extra visit from Santa or maybe his helper."

"What are you talking about?" Scott looks at me as if I'm crazy.

"I'm going to send him a secret Christmas gift."

"Hey, cool. Can I help, too?" Scott asks.

"Please, I want to be helping, also." Ashok looks at me expectantly.

"Sure. What do you think we should get him?"

Scott wants us to buy him a hand-held video game. Ashok remembers he misses the North so suggests camping stuff. I want to get him an authentic hockey jersey. Montreal Canadiens is my first choice but I'm afraid he'd guess the gift was from me and be angry. He doesn't want anyone to know he's poor.

The next day when we pool our money we realize we don't have enough to buy anything on our wish list. We settle for a hockey stick and a CD.

"How are we going to send this?" asks Ashok.

I haven't thought that far. "If we deliver it ourselves, he will know where it came from."

Ashok picks up the long skinny package and twirls it. "I do not think we can mail it."

Scott's face lights up. "I know," he squeaks. "My uncle works for a courier company. We could ask him to drop it off on his way home from work. He'd still have his uniform on."

"Would he do that?"

"Sure he would. Last April Fool's day he delivered a gag gift for someone."

* * *

"Hey, Jenkins, what's been eating you?"

The coaches are yakking outside the dressing room. As usual I'm the last one out of the place after practice.

"The team's not shaping up like I thought it would," I hear Jenkins say.

"You're joking, right? We're on a three-game winning streak for Pete's sake," Coach Eastman replies.

"You know, since we created that power line they've scored all the goals."

"And what's wrong with that?"

"Do you actually look at the game, Rob, or just the score-board? The other players are relying on them to do all the work.

They've stopped playing offensively. All they do is dump the puck down the ice. There's not much stickhandling, or passing and little or no skating going on."

"We're winning, man."

"But we're not living up to our goals for the team. They're not learning anything and they're definitely not improving their skills," the assistant coach insists.

"Sure they are. That's what practices are for."

"What's the point, Rob, if they don't get to use what they've learned in games? We always said we wanted them to stretch themselves."

Coach Eastman sighs. "Right. So, what do you want to do?"

"Make the lines equal, at least then the weak string won't get all the goals scored against it."

My stomach does a flip-flop. That's my line he's talking about. I should have known that I wasn't the only one who had noticed that.

* * *

I raise the cage face mask to wipe off the sweat running down my face. I'm pooped but happy as I head for the change room. Today I played better than I ever have before.

"Rob. What possessed you to screw with the lines?" Mr. Hartford has followed us to the dressing room after the game. "I thought we agreed that we needed a power line."

"Well it wasn't working," Coach Jenkins answers for Rob.

"Three wins is not working, but a six-one loss is?" Mick's dad asks.

Both men are speaking loud enough for it to carry into the change room. From where I'm sitting, I can see them through the open door, too. Mr. Hartford stands, hands on hips, towering over the two coaches. The assistant coach, hands balled in fists, is glaring up at him. Coach Eastman is slightly off to one side leaning against the wall.

"Yes." Jenkins nods. "For once they worked as a team."

Right on, I think. We all gave everything we had.

"Bull." Mr. Hartford voice booms into the room. "If this is what teamwork gets you, who wants it?"

"I know it might not look like it, but today everyone won."

"Today everyone won." Head shaking, eyes squinting, Mr. Hartford mocks Coach Jenkins. "Rob, tell this fool that the only winning kids understand is when they beat the other team."

"Brent, maybe he's right. We had our clocks cleaned." Coach Eastman finally says something.

"Rob, didn't you see them? They were passing. They skated their hearts out. Great stuff," Jenkins says.

It *was* great stuff. Scott passed the puck and didn't fall on his tush. Ashok almost got an assist on the goal that Sean almost got. And I swear I had wings on my feet as I tried to keep up with the play. But best of all, I got out of our end for the first time since the power line was formed.

"I know, but —" Coach Eastman hesitates.

"They still got stomped on." Mr. Hartford doesn't wait for the coach to finish.

"Granted they were outplayed. But they had some bad luck, too. In spite of everything the team as a whole played better than they've ever have before —"

"What planet did you come from?" Mick's dad cuts off the assistant coach.

"Hear me out. The great players were awesome —"

"You got that right. The poor sods had to play twice as hard to make up for the others." The giant glowers down at Coach Jenkins and steps forward crowding him. The shorter, stocky man backs up and rubs his shaved head.

"Exactly. Isn't that what we want?" He turns Hartford's argument against him. "Better players using all their skills as they compensate for the deficiencies of the weaker boys. The poorer boys learning from their stronger teammates and striving to play up to their level. I've seen it happen time and time again. My prof at college spoke about that, too."

"I should have know it was some egghead malarkey. The plain truth is kids just want to win. End of story. Ask your high-falutin teacher how good is it for kids' egos, to get whumped as we did tonight."

The whole time Coach Eastman has been glancing from one man to the other, nodding first at one then the other as the argument put forward seems logical. There is a pained look on his face.

Hartford pushes past Jenkins and finds a spot on the bench by his son. "You want a reason for why this team doesn't play like one? How about blaming all the practices some of the boys miss? Or maybe these kids just aren't committed to the game."

My friends and I get out of there as fast as we can.

"Dad, did you see my assist? Huh, did you?" I ask as we drive home.

"I sure did, buddy. Let's celebrate. This was the best game you've played yet. Slurpies?"

While I sip on my drink, I replay the game in my head. I savour the moment when Ryan scored on a pass from me — sort of.

The Flames were pressing in our end when the puck came loose. I nabbed it and got it to Ryan. By the time he reached the red line there was no one near him. Breakaway. He faked the goalie out and whipped the puck into the net. What a beaut.

* * *

I sit on our living room floor, surrounded by gifts. A warm glow from the Christmas tree fills the room. As the presents are opened, the ripping of paper echoes the fire crackling in the stone fireplace. Dad picks up the shredded wrap as fast as it arrives. Mom plays Santa and hands me the last present under the tree. I cross my fingers. Maybe this will be the hockey sweater that I'm longing for. A sly grin spreads across Grandpa's face as he watches me. I glance at the tag. It's from Mom and Dad. So why is he looking at me like that? No matter. I rip the gift open. YES. It's a Montreal Canadiens' replica jersey. Not identical to Uncle Gus' — but close enough. I pull the sweater on and admire my reflection in a silver bauble. Things don't get better than this, I think.

Grandpa still has his funny smile on his face. He starts to get up out of the rocker. My father puts his hand on Grandpa's shoulder and says, "I'll get it, Dad."

He comes back carrying a large, thin present about a metre square.

"Open it, Lee. Open it." Grandpa waves me to the package. His eyes twinkle with expectation.

I rip off the paper. Gasp. It's a huge framed collage of memorabilia from The Uncles' hockey days. In the centre is Uncle Gus' hockey jersey, washed and pressed. Surrounding it are pictures, programs and newspaper clippings about The Uncles.

"Awesome." I throw my arms around Grandpa and give him a squeeze. "Thank you, thank you, thank you."

"I noticed you spend a lot of time sifting through the stuff in Uncle Joe's chest. So…I figured you might like that for your room," he says as he hugs me back.

7

The Legion of Doom

Dolder Grand Hotel, Zurich
January 12,1935
Dear Gus,
...We received a telegram on Xmas day... We were quite thrilled...

I will close now, with best regards,
Romeo

Dolder Grand Hotel, Zurich
Saturday, January 12, 1935
Dear Ena,
...I'm glad Beef liked his Xmas gift, and did you see his Xmas card. He asked for more but that's impossible till Paris, a month from now...

Auf-weidersehn (German)
Joe

January 6, 1931
Dear Stan,
Am I glad that the holidays are over! There was no partying for me. Spent New Year's Eve alone in my room. Thought I'd have made a few good pals by now. Not knowing the language is a

definite draw back. One of the boys, a real good guy, invited me over to his family's for Xmas dinner, though. Probably shouldn't have gone because nobody 'speaked the English' so there was a lot of smiling but little conversation. I hope I didn't spoil their festivities. The food was swell, but the turkey reminded me of how much I miss Mama's cooking and how I miss the family...

Gus

As we enter the arena, Grandpa hands me a small furry object on a key chain. It's about six centimetres long. "Here, take this."

"What is it?" I yawn, then I notice the tiny claws. It's a paw. Gross.

"A rabbit's foot. For good luck. It was Uncle Romie's. He had it in his pocket when he won the Allen Cup, so, he sent it to Gus for good luck in the Stanley Cup playoffs. Seems to have done the trick. The Canadiens won that year."

I take a second look. Well, if The Uncles used it, maybe it wasn't so gross. If you think about it leather is the skin of an animal. I put the foot in my pocket. Maybe we'll win this tournament, too. Miracles can happen, right?

I yawn again. Mornings aren't my best times. What jerk would schedule a hockey game at six-forty-five on Boxing Day morning? It's our first game of the Gateway Christmas Tournament.

I shuffle into the dressing room. The bench where Ryan is sitting is mostly empty, so I plop down beside him and start to change.

"Hi," I mumble.

"Hi," he whispers back and a smile flickers across his face.

Ashok is bright and bubbly as ever when he and Scott join us. "Santa Claus, he is a very fine man. You must come and see the toys he left at our house. I am thinking, he is surely spoiling me, for I now have a hockey board game and *three* new books. Was he very, very good to you, also?"

Scott seemed to be wide awake and cheerful too. "Yup. I got the video game I wanted. And a new controller. And three CDs. Loot city. Lee, did you get that jersey you were hoping for?"

"Yeah. But sweet as that was, my grandpa did one better." I tell them about the collage.

"Cool. When do we get to see it?"

"As soon as we can work it out."

Ryan picks up his stick and starts to add another layer of tape to the end of the handle.

"That is a very nice new stick," Ashok remarked.

I give Ashok a light kick. My eyes ask, are you crazy? Do you want to give our secret away?

He just smiles and continues, "Did you get that for Christmas?"

Ryan responds to Ashok's smile. "Yes. Is it a beaut, or what? Feel how light it is. See the blade — nice and flexible." He holds it out for inspection.

Ashok pretends to examine it as if he knows what Ryan is talking about. "It is a very good stick."

Ryan nods. "It's my mystery stick. Delivered right to our door. All the tag said was Ryan Thunderchild. I thought some relative must have sent it but they all said no."

"Maybe it was Santa. He left me presents, too."

Ryan smiles. "Maybe."

I'm stunned. I don't think I've heard Ryan have a friendly chat with anyone before. Ashok seems to have connected with him. Or is it that none of us have given him half a chance at being friendly?

"Where are the coaches?" Scott squeaks.

I hadn't noticed they weren't there. I was too busy focusing on Ashok and Ryan. I look around the room. Mick Hartford is missing but the rest of the team is here and dressed to play.

"Aww, man. We'll have to forfeit the game," someone says.

"Why? We could coach ourselves. Or Ryan could," Ashok suggests.

The dressing room door opens and the coach walks in saying, "Look, I told Brent I'd stick to the plan we had at the start of the year."

"For crying out loud, Jenkins is off skiing in Jasper and I'm acting as assistant coach. That must count for something," Mr. Hartford says as he and his son follow Eastman in.

"Yes, but…" Coach Eastman hesitates, his forehead is creased in a frown.

"I'm telling you here's our chance. What Jenkins doesn't know won't hurt him. We try out our Legion of Doom line. See what they can do in a playoff-type setting."

"Well…"

"Look, the teams that enter this tournament cover the whole spectrum. If we keep the lines like Jenkins wants, we're toast. There are teams who will chew us up. If you want my advice, Rob, I say ice the strongest team."

The coach takes a deep breath and says, "Okay."

"Good man." Mr. Hartford hands the coach the clipboard he is carrying. "Here. I set up the lines as before and worked out the shift changes for you last night. I even picked up a couple extra game sheets from Gateway's office and filled them out. I thought it would save time when we're home, like in this game."

"Gee, thanks." Coach Eastman's face brightens. He calls out the lines, leads us in our rah-rah stuff, then yells, "Let's get out there. We're late."

As I grab my stick, I remember the rabbit's foot. I dig in my coat pocket to pull it out. The chain catches on my asthma inhaler. I untangle it and attach the good-luck charm to my suspenders.

We don't get much of a chance to warm up. The coach and Hartford pepper Cory with shots to give him some sort of a workout before the whistle blows to start the game.

The three amigos take their places across from the Dakota Lazers. I wonder what kind of team they are. Will they walk all over us?

Mick nabs the puck in the faceoff. He dekes around Dakota's centre, flies down the ice and weaves through their other forwards. Ryan and Sean are open by the blue line, waiting for a pass, but Mick carries the puck in himself. The Lazers double-team him. He pivots around one player before the puck's stripped off his stick by the other. The kid lobs it up to his centre. Sean poke-checks the disk loose, Ryan pounces on it, and we're back in business. Mick heads for the net, gets open and slaps his stick on the ice — calling for the pass. Ryan catapults the puck to him and he fires it at the goal. Ding. It glances off the post and falls behind the goalie.

"Hey, Clowns on Ice. Don't screw up." Mick thumps Scott's helmet as he passes him.

My line goes on. I'm nervous. Scott's finally skating securely. Ashok is faster but his passes are wild. All in all, I'm the strongest of the forwards. We just don't have a playmaker. From what I can tell, the Lazers held their own against our first string. How can we possibly keep up with them?

We can't, so we don't even try. We return to playing it safe and dumping out the puck. All we want is to make sure no damage is done on our shift. It works for the first two periods but early in the third, the line we're up against skates circles around us. In their red uniforms they zap around like the beams they're named after, popping in two quick goals to match those Mick and Ryan have wracked up.

"Geez, what can you expect from clowns?" Mick says as we settle on the bench. He puts his arm around Ryan. "We'll have to go in and clean up the mess those jokers made again, pal."

Ryan removes Mick's arm and moves up the bench a bit. He grabs a water bottle, squirts a drink and glues his eyes on the play.

The game is still tied when they take to the ice. Mick loses the faceoff and the Lazers press in our zone. Cory gloves a shot and tosses it behind the net. Sean traps it, fakes one direction, then skates out the other from behind the net. The kid makes it to the blue line and ricochets one off the boards to Mick. He stickhandles past centre — dodging first one player, then another, before having the puck knocked off his stick. Ryan snags it and gets it up to Sean. He looks for an opening, finds none so slaps it back to Ryan. Mick is in the slot waiting. Ryan's pass finds his stick and he flips it into the net.

I breathe a sigh of relief. We're back up. Then I feel sick. There's still two minutes left. My line must go on again.

As expected, the Lazers win the faceoff. They set up a shot on net. Save. Cory gets it to me and I stick with our unvoiced plan. I ice the puck. It comes right back. Again they win the faceoff. Another sizzling shot. Rebound. Again Cory blocks it. It flies my way. The buzzer goes just as I lift my stick to send the puck down the ice. Scott, Ashok and I dance a victory of hugs, high-fives and hoots.

At four o'clock we play the team from Tuxedo. In the first seconds of play Ryan's line scores. By the time their shift is over we're up three-zip. I dread stepping on the ice. We're going to screw up. I just know it.

I surprise myself and snag the puck. Scott picks up my pass and wobbles down the ice. I skate as fast as I can to give him someone to pass to. He dribbles a weak shot up to me. I'm being pressed by their centre so I dump the puck in Ashok's direction. He nabs it and works it over the red line. He passes back to me. My heart is thumping as I realize I'm going to make it into the other team's end. At least my stick, with the puck on it, makes it over their blue-line before I get poke-checked and the play heads down the rink. I turn and give chase. Ashok is with me. Scott is waiting on the other side of the red line. He teeters over to block the path of the stickhandler. The boy tries to swerve around Scott but he loses his balance. The hockey stick flies out of his grasp, slides along the ice and hits Ashok's skates. His feet shoot out from under him and he lands with a thud on his stomach. For a moment everyone stops, expecting a whistle. Ashok scrambles to his feet and Mr. Hartford waves us off. We dash for the bench.

"Let's give a hand to the three stooges," Mick says loudly. He stands up and claps as we stumble off. Some of our team-mates titter, while Mr. Hartford guffaws.

"They do not appreciate my fancy skating. Could Emanuel Sandhu, the figure skater, have done that? I am surely thinking, no. A triple klutz like that is not an easy thing to do. Mine was worth a five-point-nine do you not think?" Ashok jokes, washing away my embarrassment.

I reach up my jersey and stroke the rabbit's foot. I don't care what they think; I'm having a great game. So, I'm just going to keep playing the way I have. If The Uncles or Coach Jenkins were there, they would know I'm giving it all I've got.

Dad and Grandpa can see it. They give me the thumbs-up as we head for the change room.

* * *

WINNIPEG EVENING TRIBUNE
Friday, December 8, 1933
...The captain, Rivers, set off the spark. Before ten minutes were over he had scored two beautiful goals, on passes from his brother Joe and Lamay.
The action was picking up at a rapid rate and other players beside Romeo began to catch the spirit of the things...

I'm high as a kite. The Uncles' lucky charm is doing its magic. We've won our first three games. In the last two, Scott, Ashok and I got to really play, not just dump the puck out of our end. I skated, stickhandled and even took a couple shots on goal. *That* was sweeter than the scores of five-nothing and eight to two that our team wracked up.

"Okay, boys. Now we're going to be tested —" Coach Eastman starts his pep talk.

Hartford interrupts, "Till now it's been as easy as slipping on ice."

I wonder what game he was watching when we played the Lazers.

"The Saint Norbert Storm are a tough bunch. They've won all their games, too, but not because of namby-pamby opposition. Luckily we have our Legion of Doom line, that's you, you, and you." Hartford points at Mick, Sean and Ryan. He has taken over. "You're going to give us one hundred and ten percent. The rest of you are going to play defensively. DUMP OUT THAT PUCK. Got it? Now lets get out there."

"What about our cheer?" Ryan asks.

"Huh? Oh, yeah." Hartford turns to Eastman.

The coach leads us but there's no power in our voices.

The whole first period we're scrambling. The play is up and down the rink when Ryan's line is on the ice. When the rest of us are playing, the only thing going up the rink is the iced puck.

"Good work, guys. We're hanging in there," Eastman says between periods.

"But we need a break if we hope to win. Mick, think you can take a dive and make it look like a trip?" Hartford asked.

"Doug, that's not the kind of thing we want to teach the boys. Is it?" Eastman is hesitant.

"We need a break, so we're making one. It's not like I'm asking anyone to take a penalty. Don't sweat it."

Early in the second period Mick fakes a trip. The Storm get a penalty and are one man short. We get our power play. Ryan is able to capitalize on it and we're up one to zero.

The Storm don't take too kindly to that. During our shift they put the screws to us. In the last seconds their centre makes a run for the net. I skate into his path to block his progress. As he dekes around me, he lifts his elbow and nearly takes my head off. Penalty. Two minutes for elbowing.

As I stagger off the ice for the line change, Hartford is blocking our third line from stepping on the rink.

"Geez, Rob, we ice the best line for the job. We've got a power play, the only logical choice is the Legion of Doom line. Right?"

"I guess…"

"Okay. Mick get your line on the ice. We don't want a delay of game penalty," Hartford yells.

The three amigos do us proud and we're up two-zip. The Storm are steaming and they get chippy. We get ticked and take penalties, too. By the end of the period we're tied.

We're still tied two-two in the last couple minutes of the game. Hartford sends Mick's line on again. The guys work their butts off and it pays big time when Sean drills one into the five-hole. I hoot and holler our victory but my mind is a jumble of thoughts. We won. I didn't mess up. Could it be the rabbit's foot?

"Got to hand it to you, Doug. You know how to coach a winning game." Eastman and Hartford are all smiles as they thump each others backs.

Coaching, smoaching. By the time the round robin is done we're in the playoffs and I know it's because of The Uncles' rabbit's foot.

* * *

"The Gateway Flyers are your worst nightmare. They're on home turf, too." Hartford's words ring in my head as I faceoff.

No kidding. His Legion of Doom have met their match. Our line is going to get creamed.

The puck drops and the Flyers are in business. I try and stop their assault, but no luck. I feel like a fat bumble bee buzzing aimlessly — achieving nothing. Our end is a swarm of orange sweaters as the Flyers pepper Cory with shots. Four. Five. Six. They can't all miss. Or can they? The puck finally zings off the goalposts and over the glass. As I shuffle off the ice I stroke the rabbit's foot and give thanks to its power.

I dread each shift. Before I step on the ice I wrap my fingers around the foot and pray I won't make a big mistake. The Flyers have five goals, two of them scored against the Legion of Doom.

When the final buzzer goes, the Flyers have won twelve to three.

Mr. Hartford slams the change room door behind the team, silencing our chatter.

"That was pathetic! My son's line carried this team to the quarter-finals. They played their hearts out today. So where were the rest of you bozos?"

"Doug, easy off —"

"Heck, no. They need to hear this. They sit on their hands and let the skilled players do all the work. They act as if practice is optional. Show up only if they feel like it. If they had more commitment to the team, think how far we could have gone. They disgust me." He slams out of the room.

Eastman clears his throat, is about to speak but changes his mind and leaves, too.

We're crushed by the telling-off we've just got. The room is silent as we change.

"I am thinking, the lucky charm you have hidden under your shirt did not work today," Ashok whispers as I take off my sweater.

"Are you kidding? We're the only line that didn't get scored on," I whisper back. I unhook the foot and stroke it.

"Maybe, sucker, that's because they didn't take time to set up plays when you jokers were on. It was one big shot-fest," Mick sneers.

"But they still didn't score," I say. My line beams like the clowns he takes us for.

8

Man-makers

March 2, 1931
Dear Stan,
I'm down in the dumps. Still haven't made any close pals. I've learned a bit of French but not enough to really get to know a fellow. The big shots don't want much to do with a nineteen-year-old rookie, so fat chance I'll be chummy with the English-speaking guys anytime soon. What's a kid who grew up with four brothers and lots of friends to do alone in the big city? Have to snap out of this blue mood. The team is flying but I'm tired of living out of suitcases, long bus rides and watching hockey from the bench. I miss being in the game....

Gus

You're kidding? Right?" Jenkins' voice penetrates into the dressing room.

It's the first practice after the holidays. I'm early. Mom had to go pick Dad up because his car died in the cold. I huddle tighter into the corner I'm sitting in and try not to eavesdrop.

"Brent, I think this is for the best. They got to the quarter-finals. Imagine. And it wasn't only because of our power line either. Even that Rivers kid had some shots on net during the tournament," Coach Eastman replies.

My ears prick up when I hear my name.

"I don't like it, Rob. But if you're not giving me a choice, at least promise me we'll play a strong defense line with the weaker kids. I want them to have a hope of touching the puck, even if they can't nab it themselves. The defense will be able to check and pass it up to them. Okay?"

"No problem. It's settled then. We're keeping Doug's Legion of Doom line."

Kids and their parents start to dribble in. There's a buzz of chatter as we get dressed. Adults drift out and coaches bustle in.

"Way to go, guys! Wish I could have been there to see you play." Coach Jenkins is high as he laces up a skate.

Mr. Hartford is lacing up skates, too. When all the other parents left the dressing room he stayed behind. "I don't know what you're cheering about. They flubbed the quarter-finals big time."

"Yeah. So? They went way farther the we ever expected. Maybe we've been underestimating them," Jenkins replies.

"Or maybe I just know how to coach a team to win, boy."

Coach Jenkins scowls and jerks at his laces. "Let's hit the ice, guys."

We don't break into our groups because a third of the kids are missing, but we follow the same routine. I give it all I've got. If Coach Eastman thinks I did all right in the tournament, I must be improving. At the end of practice I'm mush. My legs are rubber and I'm breathing hard. Just an A-one workout — not an asthma attack? Of course not, I chuckle, reassuring myself.

I move in slow mo as I change. Everyone's long gone by the time I pull on my hiking boots.

"Flipping poor showing, if you ask me. Like I've said before, the majority of these kids have no commitment to the game, what...so...ever." Mr. Hartford and the coaches are hanging out by the canteen, knocking back cold drinks.

I move to the front door to wait for Dad and I stare at the blowing snow. Trying to block out their voices, I concentrate on the whistling of the wind. But my attention is drawn back to them.

"I'd bench each one of those wussies a period or two for each practice they missed, if it was up to me," he continues.

"A good thing it's not. That's harsh, don't you think?" Coach Jenkins says.

"Heck, no. A little consequence for their actions, and boy-o-boy, they'd make more of an effort to show up." Mick's dad takes a swig from his drink.

"Come on now, this is only house league hockey," Jenkins chuckles.

"Oh. For crying out loud. House league. Triple A. It's all the same. You do what it takes to field a winning team."

I wish adults would stop scrapping in public.

"They're only kids, for heaven's sake, looking to have fun."

"BULL. It's softies like you that are ruining hockey. Look how we're being humiliated on the world stage. Take your theories and the powder-puffs and go teach them figure skating. Leave hockey for the men." Hartford crumples his pop can, chucks it into the garbage and yells, "Mick, we're out of here."

Coach Jenkins uses a serviette to pull out Hartford's can from the garbage. He tosses it into the recycling bin. "What's Hartford doing suiting up for practice and interferring with the coaching, anyway?"

Same question I've been asking myself.

"Brent, maybe we can learn something from him," the coach replies.

"What? That good players play well and weak players don't? Give me a break, Rob."

"He did a great job in the tournament. He feels he's earned a spot on the coaching team. I think so, too."

I am so glad when Dad pulls up.

"Hey, buddy, What's up? You're sucking air. Asthma attack?" Dad places his hands on my shoulders and takes a closer look.

I'm still having a bit of trouble breathing. Asthma? Na, it can't be, this is my good season. But it sure feels like it.

"Maybe I'm getting sick," I answer. That can bring on an asthma attack, too.

"Got your inhaler?" my dad asks.

I pat my pocket in answer — Mom insists I carry it at all times.

"Maybe you should take your medication, just in case," Dad says, so I pull out the tiny canister, shake it and take a puff.

* * *

"Where were you last night?" I yell to Scott the morning after our second practice of the new year. I can't keep the concern out of my voice.

"At Grandma Kozusko's. For Ukrainian Christmas. Why?" He jogs up to Ashok and me as we huddle by the school entrance, trying to keep warm.

"You're going to be benched a period," I say.

"What for?" He blinks behind his thick lenses.

"Missing practice."

"Yeah, right." Scott laughs.

"Oh, yes. It is for certain. The coaches were having themselves a very great argument. I was not liking it at all." Ashok frowns.

"No way." Scott's eyes bug out of his head.

"Yup, you missed quite a show. Coach Jenkins and Mick's

dad were arguing again. Five kids were no-shows. Mr. Hartford took a hissy fit about it. Got Coach Eastman ticked about it, too. He went on and on about lack of respect for the coaches. 'We show up no matter how cold it is.'" I mimic Hartford.

"Mr. Hartford, he is believing, that the kids were not there because it was bitterly cold."

"Then he started to whine how the *wussies* got the same ice time as everyone else and how unfair it was to the kids who made every practice. He wanted them benched."

"Mr. Jenkins, he was not liking it. But Mr. Eastman said he was agreeing with the benching, so, Mr. Jenkins, he leaves."

"He didn't say anything. But, boy, was he steamed."

I let my mind linger on the memory of the practice. It was a bad night all around. The shortness of breath. The tightness of my chest, as if King Kong was sitting on it. Having to take my inhaler twice before there was any relief.

Mom dragged me to Dr. Klassen's the next morning. She figured the combination of extreme cold and hard exercise was the cause.

No longer can I deny that the practices are resulting in asthma attacks. I'll have to make sure I take my inhaler before each one. No more healthy season. What a drag.

* * *

"I have a complaint from the Winakwa coach." The ref skates up to our bench at the end of the first period during the next game. "He says you're not playing all your players."

"Only the ones that were benched for missing practice, Ref. They'll be playing next period. Should we have informed you?"

Mr. Hartford is so syrupy I could puke.

"Na, that's okay. Just checking."

"Sour grapes," Mick's dad mumbles to Coach Eastman as the ref skates away. Both men laugh. Coach Jenkins glares at them from the other side of the bench.

We're up by two. With five players benched, the Legion of Doom and my line have been playing every second shift. I feel sorry for Scott and the other boys.

The second period starts. Ryan's line dominates but doesn't score. We have a great shift, too. As we get off the ice, Scott's line prepares to go on.

"Hold on there a minute. The Legion of Doom will keep taking every second shift. You'll go on after them, okay?" Mr. Hartford says.

"Like, heck! Rob?" the assistant coach is seething.

Coach Eastman just shrugs.

"Mick, get your line out there." Mr. Hartford looks at Jenkins and smirks.

The assistant coach slams the gate closed behind Sean and sits down.

"I am not liking this very much," Ashok whispers to me.

I know exactly how he feels, my stomach's a blender. The bad feeling of the adults hangs like a storm cloud over the bench. Coach Jenkins heads for the dressing room as soon as the final buzzer goes. There is little cheering, even though we win four to two.

The assistant coach is waiting for Coach Eastman at the change room door. "Rob, when we started, I thought we believed in the same things. Fair play. Equal playing time. Building skills. And most important, the kids having fun. I don't see that happening, so, I'm throwing in the towel."

"Brent, are you nuts? You'll fail the course, if you quit the team now."

"Hey, don't worry about me. I'm a big boy. I can take care of myself. Take care, guys. I'll miss you." Coach Jenkins waves at us then turns back to the coach before leaving. "Good luck with your sidekick. Or are you his?"

"Don't sweat it, kid." Mr. Hartford puts his arm around Coach Eastman's shoulder. "Good riddance."

When I tell them, Dad and Mom aren't happy about Coach Jenkins' quitting.

"That's too bad, buddy. I know how much you liked him."

* * *

"What did I tell you? Give them a consequence. See? It's cold enough to freeze the fish in the Red, but the wussies are all here." Mr. Hartford grins as he walks into the change room with Coach Eastman.

"The jerk's crazy. It's not Ukrainian Christmas, or exams or anything. That's why we're all here. We're not wussies." Scott whispers.

"I've been giving this some thought, and I think it's time to get them in condition for the playoffs. Well, Rob?" Hartford pulls his skates out of his son's bag.

"Yeah. Maybe…" Eastman bobs his blond head sideways. "What did you have in mind?"

"For starters, man-makers." He turns to speak to the team. "We need to toughen up you wimps. We'll be starting each practice with ten laps. Then sprints across the rink, dropping at the red line to do push-ups and sit-ups. Let's say we start out easy. Ten minute's worth. Now hit the ice."

I skate around the rink with Ashok and Scott, wishing I was in a nice warm indoor arena. But no such luck, all our practices are outdoors.

"I am thinking, that last practice, it was like the tropics compared to this." Ashok's brown eyes peer out from behind his red balaclava. He fans the white puffs of breath as he speaks. We're in the midst of Winnipeg's inevitable January cold snap.

Ryan and the crew lap us for the second time.

Mr. Hartford glides up to us, "Move it you slow pokes. This isn't a stroll in the park."

He falls in line behind us, so close on our tails that we are forced to pick up our pace to avoid being bowled over. Every now and then he yells, "Come on. Come on."

Ashok gains a small lead on us. Slowly I pull away from Scott, too. I lose count of the laps and hope my friends are keeping track. When I see Ashok pull over and stop, I follow him. I lean on the boards, panting. I've barely caught my breath when a whistle shrills.

"Line up at that end. Let's go. Lets go," Hartford yells. "Okay. Sprint to the middle, drop and give me twenty push-ups. Get up and dash the rest of the way. On the return trip, at the red line you do twenty sit-ups. And repeat till I tell you to stop. Got it?"

Eastman is leaning on the boards watching. Why has he let the jerk take over, I wonder?

Hartford blows his whistle again and I concentrate on the task at hand. By the third rep I'm breathing hard. On the fifth trip my legs are turning to gummy worms and I'm short of breath. The ape is sitting on my chest. I force myself to complete the push-ups before heading into the clubhouse for my inhaler.

I sit in the change room until my breathing eases a bit. On the way back out I gulp a cold one from the drinking fountain. Water always seems to help.

By the time I get on the ice, the man-makers are finished and the coaches are putting the team through a stickhandling drill. I fall in line beside Scott.

"Are you okay?" he asks.

I nod as I pick up Ryan's pass and maneuver the puck through the maze of pylons.

At the end of practice I'm still not a hundred percent, so changing is a slow, drawn-out process. As usual, I'm the last one in the room except for the coaches. They're pouring over stats from the league. Mr. Thunderchild pokes his head in and asks to speak with Mr. Hartford. The two men leave the room. A few minutes later Mr. Thunderchild is back.

"Excuse me, Coach, there's something that's bothering me. I've noticed my son's line been playing more than their share of the —"

"Mr. Thunderchild, you should speak to Doug Hartford if you've got a concern. Remember we set up that hierarchy at the first practice." Eastman puts his clipboard into his sports bag.

"I just did but —"

I want to be out of there, so I try to move faster, but I feel like I'm wearing a lead wet suit.

"Rob, you go. I'll handle it." Hartford is back. He waits for the coach to leave, then turns on Ryan's dad. "Look. Like I told you, fair or not, we follow the rules the way they're written. Haven't we switched about every two minutes? If they intended to say each line must play an equal amount of time, oh well. They should have spelled it out. And what the heck are you bellyaching for? Your kid's the one who is benefitting." The ogre sees me lacing up my boots. "What are you doing? Snooping? Pick up your things and get your butt out of here."

I throw my stuff into my hockey bag and scramble out of the room.

9

Consequences

THE PORT ARTHUR NEWS-CHRONICLE
Tuesday, April 14, 1931
...Gus Rivers, the well-liked boy from Winnipeg, hasn't figured strongly in the Stanley Cup playoffs, but when Howie Morenz was on the shelf near the close of the schedule, it was the same Gus Rivers who jumped into the breach and played fine hockey...

April 9, 1931
Dear Stan,
...Boy what a game! The Black Hawks put up a valiant fight but we pulled off the win. I'm almost giddy about winning the Stanley Cup again. I've kept Romie's old rabbit's foot in my pocket since he sent it. It sure has brought our team luck.

About stopping in Port Arthur to visit on my way back to Winnipeg, our favourite gal nixed that. Mama wants me to make tracks for home so I think I'll oblige her. Romie and I figure we'll drive up and visit you this summer instead...

Gus

"This is surely a very good day. My aunty Sharmila is here, all the way from Bombay. Look, up there beside my father." Ashok points into the stands at a lady wearing a navy parka over an orange sari. She waves vigorously at him. He turns back to me, grinning. "And, Mr. Hartford, he is away."

He and Mick haven't shown up and we're already on the ice warming up. I do a lunge to stretch my leg muscles. I haven't been able to do too much skating in my backyard since the freezing cold set in. My asthma has been getting in the way. Thank goodness the games are played in warm indoor arenas. I have no problems here.

"Hey, Eastman." Two of the men who ran the A-level try-outs are leaning over the boards.

The coach skates over to them and shakes hands. "You slumming or what?"

"Actually, we're here to raid your team," the short bald guy says.

"Forget it, you had your chance." The coach laughs and the others join in.

"Seriously though, we're here checking out that Thunder-child kid. Saw him play in the Gateway tournament." The tall thin one points at Ryan as he flies by.

"Quite impressive," his partner adds.

"His whole line is," Coach Eastman says.

"Yeah, but Sean Chan has turned us down every year and there are issues with the Hartford kid. He's saddled with an interferring dad. No A-level coach will touch him." He rubs his bald spot.

"We're kicking ourselves for cutting Thunderchild, though." The skinny guy shakes his head.

Bart was wrong. Just like I thought, Ryan's dad wasn't the pushy parent.

"It was a toss-up between him and another boy. We went with the guy we knew. Kyle's played Triple A with us for three seasons," his friend says.

"But he doesn't hold a candle to Thunderchild. I'm surprised no one else picked him up. I guess they thought the same as us — unknown quantity. That often happens to the new kid on the block." Skinny is following Ryan with his eyes as he speaks.

"But, you can kiss him goodbye for next season, all the A-level coaches are hoping to snap him up." Suddenly shorty gets a startled look on his face. He elbows his partner and nods his head in the direction of the arena doors. The Hartfords are striding toward us.

"Talk to you later. Got to go." They wave and take off as if they're running from something.

"Stupid alarm didn't go." Mr. Hartford chucks Mick's bag into our box. "What did those two jerks want?"

"Just scouting."

"Humph. They wouldn't know talent if it skated under their noses. Imagine, those idiots cut Mick!"

I pull away from the boards, hoping to get in a couple of warm-up laps before the whistle goes. No such luck; that's what I get for eavesdropping.

Ryan's line is in the groove. They skate circles around the Notre Dame Hounds, keeping them hemmed in their own end. By their third shift, they've got the Hounds ticked. They're used to being top dog and they don't like being down by two in the first period one bit.

Next period, they start to bump us around, even while they're walking all over our line. Although I'm as big as they are, I don't appreciate the contact. I stay out of trouble by getting rid of the puck as fast as I can.

Well into the third period, Ashok still hasn't caught on. He sweeps up the puck from along the boards and shuffle-flies over our blue line. The humongous Notre Dame centre goes after him. I don't know what the hulk is thinking because he body-checks Ashok. The small boy goes sailing in the air and lands splayed out on the ice. Everyone freezes for an instant. Then, as if the screech from the stands has broken a spell, we rush toward the kid and the ref blows his whistle. I get there first.

"Are you okay?"

Ashok lifts his head and nods. White teeth flash behind his face mask. The nutty kid's smiling.

"I am thinking, that must have been one very fine flying camel going into a spread eagle. Emanuel Sandhu will be jealous."

I reach down and help him up. The arena erupts in clapping as he gets to his feet.

"I am hoping Aunty Sharmila is thinking, I am one tough hockey player," he says as we skate to the bench.

"Or a crazy one. Why didn't you just dump the puck?"

"Then how would my favourite aunty know how fast I can skate and how well I stickhandle?"

"Couldn't you have shown her at the practices?"

"I will not be making the next two practices. My family has big plans for us while Aunty is here."

When the Legion of Doom gets on the ice they're on fire. Ashok's hit has riled up our whole team. They fly up the ice, ending the power play in seconds. Then just to rub Notre Dame's noses in it, they knock another one in the net just before the buzzer ends the game.

* * *

"Rivers. Prasad. Don't bother suiting up. You're benched for the game." Mr. Hartford strides into the dressing room before our game with Windsor.

I'm stunned. Ashok freezes, one arm in and the other out of his sweatshirt.

"The whole game?" Scott squeaks in surprise.

"What are you sticking your nose in for?" the ogre snaps at him, then he turns back to us. "Might as well put your coats back on and scram. This should teach you to miss practices. You knew there'd be consequences."

I lace up my hiking boots, zip up my hockey bag and head out the door with Ashok. I hate Hartford.

"You're going the wrong way, boys. Room three. Move it; you're late." Coach Eastman points to the way we've just come.

We hesitate. He puts his hands on Ashok's shoulders and turns him around.

"But, Mr. Eastman, Mr. Hartford, he is telling us that we are not to be playing this game," he explains.

The coach laughs. "A language problem, no doubt."

"No it's not. He's benched us," I say.

"Must be some mistake. Come on, let's go clear this up." He leads us back into the room. "Doug, these kids have some crazy idea that they're benched for the game."

"You bet they are. Consequences. That's the only way they'll learn."

"Agreed, but a whole game? That's a bit much don't you think? Let them suit up and play at least one, if not two periods."

"Prasad's missed two practices and Rivers has been wimping out on the man-makers. He hasn't completed a single practice — from beginning to end — since we started them."

"Ashok told us his aunt was in town so he wouldn't be there. And you know Lee has asthma, for Pete's sake."

"And…? Rob, don't go soft on me now. Remember we're toughening them up. Look, have I ever steered you wrong?"

"No, but…" Coach Eastman weakens.

"Didn't I take the team to the quarter-finals?" Hartford asks and I know we've lost.

"Sorry, guys." Coach Eastman shrugs. "We'll see you next practice."

"Good man. They were warned."

Hah, some warning, Old Hartford never once said I'd have to sit out a game. As we walk out to the stands, I let my mind wander back to that last practice.

"Don't think I haven't seen you wimping out of the man-makers ever since they've started. You've been sneaking into the clubhouse and returning after they're done." The giant loomed in the change room door, blocking my path.

"I wasn't sneaking off the ice. I just needed to come in and use my inhaler."

"Boy, you wussies are good. What do you do? Stay up nights, thinking up excuses to get you off the hook from putting out one hundred percent?"

"But, Mr. Hartford, my asthma *has* been acting up lately."

"Yeah, right. And your little friend is really here today wearing an invisible cloak. Give me a break. Believe me, there will be consequences." He stalked away before I could say anything more in my defense.

I snap back to earth when Dad says, "What's up, buddy? Did you forget something at home?"

"No. The creep, Hartford, has benched me because I didn't finish the man-makers."

"Did you tell him you were having breathing problems?"

"Yeah. But he doesn't care. He thinks I'm a wuss who just can't handle the workout. Ashok can't play because he couldn't make the practices when his aunt was in town. It's so not fair."

"You're right, Lee, but it's typical hockey mentality. That's why I never missed the sport. How about I take you out for breakfast? Maybe the Prasads would like to join us?"

"Can't we watch the game first?" I ask.

Ashok says to his dad, "I am not wanting to go yet, also, Father."

We decide to stay and cheer the team on.

10

Ten Short Minutes

WINNIPEG FREE PRESS
Thursday, January 5, 1956
WHAT'S AILING JUNIOR HOCKEY? FORMER PLAYERS GIVE
THEIR VIEWS

by Ralph Bagley
...Return to the fundamentals of hockey was (Romeo) Rivers'
solution to the problem. "Teach them to stickhandle, teach them
to pass properly, teach them to play positional hockey and
backcheck and teach them to skate hard and fast..."

October 11, 1931
Dear Stan,
Finally feeling in tip-top condition. Hart's been putting us
through some really tough practices. The starting line are as
good as they've ever been so I'm only getting a shift here or there.
Had a good one in our last game in Boston. Lou Peiri, owner of
the Rhode Island Reds, came down to the dressing room and we
had a nice chat. He seems like a real nice guy. He voiced my
greatest fears — thinks I'm a great puckster but figures it will
take a long time to break into the starting squad. He made me an
offer to join his outfit. I think he was joshing but I'm not sure...
Gus

I pull my helmet on over my balaclava, snap the face mask shut and step on the ice. I skate the laps in long gliding strokes, free as a snowy owl on a cold winter's night. And it is icy cold — minus twenty-six Celsius, but with the wind chill it's like negative thirty. Most coaches would have cancelled practice, but not Eastman and Hartford. Dad suggested I stay home. No way. I'm going to show Hartford how wrong he is. I get lapped even by Scott. But no problem, this time I'm determined to pace myself. I pull up along the boards, last man in, still feeling strong. Hartford whistles for us to line up for the man-makers. I take a deep breath.

"I can do this," I say to myself. "It's only ten short minutes."

When the whistle shrieks, I take off, keeping pace with Ashok. At the red line I drop and do the push-ups — slowly, rhythmically. Nineteen. Twenty. I pop up, sprint to the end of the rink, turn and return to the red line. I lie flat on my back and jackknife into a sit-up. By the fourth trip down the rink, I've slowed down a bit. Ashok is ahead of me and Scott is skating at my side. He gives me a thumbs-up as we sprint to the boards. We turn in unison and make for the red line. Flat on our backs once more, we do sit-ups. My breathing is laboured. I need to concentrate on the task. Fif...teen... Six...teen... In the edge of my vision, Scott gets up and starts his sprint. Nine...teen... Twen...ty... King Kong has taken his seat and it feels like he's gained weight. I slowly get to my feet and skate to the end and back again. Wheezes punctuate my breathing as I stretch out on the ice and do push-ups. Push, push, push. Up. Twelve. Drop. Push, push, push. Up. Thirteen. Drop.

"That's it, Rivers. You can do it. You've got your ancestors' blood in your veins." Ryan is beside me on the ice doing sit-ups — three for every one of my push-ups. He stays till I'm on my feet, then skates in the opposite direction.

What trip is this? I've lost count. I skate through molasses. Without knowing how I got there, I'm back at the red line. I lie on my stomach on the ice and listen to my breathing for a moment. Wheeze...wheeze. Wheeze...wheeze. Wheeze, WHEEZE, wheeze. Wheeze...wheeze. I start to push up. My arms refuse to obey me. I rest for a moment, then try again and my head raises a hairbreadth off the ice surface. I pu...sh and rise another centimetre.

I can hear Scott, Ashok and Ryan yelling, "Lee... Lee... Lee." Cheering me on?

I give it all I've got and my body rises as if I'm being lifted. YES. My hands and feet leave the ice. Crud, I *am* being lifted. Dad has his arms around my waist and is carrying me off the rink.

"NO...O," I yell but no sound comes out. I struggle to be released but my movements are feeble. Exhausted, I give up and let my father buckle me into the van.

"Here," someone says and an arm hands Dad my coat and boots. Dad pulls out my inhaler and helps me take a puff.

"Go. I'll take care of the rest," the voice speaks again.

* * *

I lie on the examining table, eyes closed, smelling the medicinal odour of the emergency room. The all-too-familiar scene plays itself out. The doctor walks in, listens to my lungs and orders a mask of Ventolin. He hands my dad a prescription for the steroid pills.

As he opens the door to leave, Mom pushes her way in. "What happened? Is he all right?"

"The doctor said he's doing fine. No need to admit him, but he collapsed at the practice," Dad answers. Collapsed?

"No, no. I was doing push-ups."

"Push-ups? The whistle blew. Didn't you hear it? The kids

cleared the ice but you just lay there on the red line. And your friends kept calling to you but you wouldn't move."

Whistle? Could that have been that strange loud wheeze I'd heard? And the boys cheering me on, that was just calls of worry?

Dad turns to Mom. "I had to carry him off the rink. That stupid Hartford just went on with the practice. At least Eastman had the decency to pick up Lee's stick and bring it to the van. If I didn't have to rush him here, I'd have torn a strip off both of them."

The nurse walks in and loads the Ventolin into the medication dispenser. She uncoils the hose attached to it, places the mask over my nose and mouth and turns on the pump. "Try and relax. You'll be tip-top in no time." She pats me on the head and leaves.

"So much for another illustrious Rivers' hockey career," Mom says to my dad.

I want to ask her what she means, but the mask covering my nose and mouth prevents me from speaking.

I'm so tired I can hardly keep my eye open as we drive home. "I'm…not…quitting." I yawn around the words.

"Let's not worry about that right now, buddy." Dad smiles at me in the rear view mirror.

In the morning, my breathing is pretty good but I can't go to school even if I want to. I'm so tired and weak that I sleep the day away.

When I'm ready to get up, Mom helps me to the family room and makes me comfortable on the sofa. Handing me a mug of chicken soup, she sits down on the rug beside me. She grabs a section of the newspaper from Dad and starts to read. I channel surf for a couple of minutes but nothing can stop my mom's comments of the night before from playing over and over in my head.

"What did you mean last night, about my hockey career?" I ask.

She looks up from the newspaper spread out in front of her.

"Well, obviously, after last night you must realize that hockey is not for you."

"You figure I should give up hockey? Why? Just because my asthma acted up? In spring you don't tell me to stop breathing? Just doing *that* in the pollen-filled air is asthma causing."

"For heaven's sake, Lee, now you're being ridiculous."

"No I'm not. Lots of athletes — even hockey players — have asthma and they don't quit. They manage it. That's what Dr. Klassen says. I didn't manage it — that's all."

"That's not true and you know it."

"Maybe, but it wasn't the hockey. It was the man-makers. And the freezing cold."

"And those are the things you have no control over."

"But the cold won't last forever. Then I'll be fine." My voice is shrill and anxious.

"You're joking? Those turkeys pushed you through a workout that put your health in jeopardy and you want to go back for more?" Mom's voice is as shrill as mine.

"YES."

She turns to Dad. "You talk some sense into him."

He lowers his paper. "Lee, your mother's right, you know. The hockey is affecting your health. This is the first time you've had asthma attacks in the winter."

"Dad. Please don't make me quit. Not now. You said the whistle went. You know what that means? I completed the man-makers. It's the combination of them and the extreme cold that did me in. This freezing weather won't last for ever. Please, Dad, please. I'll take it easy until then."

Before he can reply the doorbell rings.

Dad ushers Ryan and Mr. Thunderchild into the room. He is carrying my hockey bag in one hand. "Look who dropped by for a visit."

Mom scrambles to pick up the papers on the floor. "Sit. Sit. What can I get you? Coffee? Tea? Soft drink?"

"Black coffee sounds great." Mr. Thunderchild lowers himself into an upholstered chair.

"What can I get you, Ryan? We have cola, root beer and ginger ale," Mom asks as she hands Ryan's dad his drink. Ryan is standing beside his dad's chair, looking at his feet.

Ryan raises his eyes to my mom and says, "Root beer, please," then lowers his head again.

"Hey, Ryan, come sit here." I pat the sofa cushion beside me.

He shuffles over, hesitantly, nothing like the bully we've taken him for.

"How are you doing, kid? The last time I saw you, you were in rough shape," Mr. Thunderchild asks.

"I'm okay." I'm not a hundred percent but anything beats not being able to breathe.

"Next practice you should take it a little easier."

"There won't be a next practice," Mom says.

Mr. Thunderchild's head snaps in my direction. "I didn't know he was that ill."

"I'm not. They won't let me go back," I blurt out.

Ryan's dad's face reddens. "Oh," he says.

Mom's face is red, too. "Well, the way they're pushing the kids... We just can't take a chance with Lee's health."

"No, no, but it's too bad. He seems to enjoy playing."

"The season started out so well. Good exercise, lots of fun, great concept of sport..." Dad shakes his head. "But it's slowly gone downhill."

"Yup. Ever since the Christmas tournament and Hartford sticking his nose in the coaching."

"Jenkins seemed to have a head on his shoulders. I miss that kid."

"I think that was the problem — Eastman and Jenkins both being so young. It worried me from day one. Not that they would do a poor job coaching, but that they wouldn't be able to stand up to the pushy parents. At first I was so glad that Hartford had volunteered to field the problems."

"Me, too. I figured no one could intimidate that giant. Who knew *he'd* be the pushy parent?"

We all laugh.

"But, seriously, we shouldn't let them drive your boy out of hockey."

Way to go, Mr. Thunderchild. I cross my fingers and pray.

A frown creases Mom's forehead. "Excuse me, but it's my son's health that's at stake."

"Exactly, ma'am. I think we should fight for his right to play without putting his health at risk. Don't you? After all, this is the recreational league."

Dad says, "He's right, dear, we can't give up without even trying."

Go, Dad, go.

"I don't know…" Mom hesitates.

"We'll talk to Eastman when Hartford isn't around. Maybe make some kind of a compromise. If he won't listen? Well at least we tried. What do you say?"

"No compromise, then he quits, okay?" Mom stares into Dad's eyes until he nods.

YES.

The doorbell rings again. Scott and Ashok have come to check out how I am.

"Why don't you take your friends into your room?" my mother suggests.

At the entrance to my room, Ryan stops dead in his tracks. He stares at the framed memorabilia from Grandpa.

"Fantastic, isn't it?" Scott squeaks.

Ryan just nods and walks slowly up to it. He runs his hands over the glass — stopping every now and then to read something. He points to Uncle Romie in the picture of the 1932 Canadian Olympic hockey team. "He got a gold medal? Have you seen it?"

I nod. "Grandpa's got it and one from the World Cup in Davos, Switzerland. Uncle Joe's I think. I'll ask him to bring them to show us the next time he visits."

"Excellent." Scott's blue eyes twinkle.

"I am thinking, that that would be most wonderful." Ashok rubs his brown hands together.

"I wish I could see them," Ryan says wistfully.

"Of course, I meant you, too."

For the first time I see a smile really light up his face.

He turns back to the framed mementos and traces the outline of Uncle Gus' sweater.

"Ever since you did that project on your uncles, I've wanted to ask you stuff. I tried to talk to you a bunch of times, but —"

"But I cut you off. Right?"

He nods and returns to tracing the hockey sweater. Guilt washes over me.

"My uncle Johnny would have played in the NHL someday. He was awesome. He played for the OCN Blizzards. They said the scouts were looking at him."

"So, why is it, that he is not going to?" Ashok asks.

"He died."

Silence settles upon us like a led weight. I'm so relieved when Mom comes in to tell Ryan that his dad is ready to leave.

11

Just a Fair Shake

THE TORONTO DAILY STAR
Monday, February 15, 1932
by Lou Marsh
...And tall "Hack" Simpson...the second string forward line of the Canadian team, and Romeo Rivers, big, powerful left-wing speed demon of the first line are the outstanding individual heroes of the most desperate and thrill-producing battle Canada ever had to put up to retain unbroken the string of Canadian victories at the Winter Olympiads...

February 27, 1932
Dear Stan,
Congratulate Romie for me when you see him. Mama must be bragging to everyone about her boy's gold medal.

Morenz, Joliat and the boys are having a stellar season. Doesn't look like they're going to slow down any time soon. And as long as that's the case I'll be biding my time on the bench. Sometimes I wonder if I made the right decision going pro. The money's okay but it doesn't make up for not getting to play much. If I had stayed in Winnipeg I'd have seen a lot of ice time and I could have been at the Olympics with Romie. Enough whining. I should be grateful to have won two Stanley Cups!

Gus

"Must be my lucky day," I say to Ryan, sitting beside me on the snowbank. I open my mouth wide to catch a snowflake. All day long the opal grey skies have shed big fluffy ones, but by six-thirty the flurry has slowed to a trickle.

"Why?" he asks.

"Well, your dad talked my parents into letting me come today. And the cold snap has broken, so it won't be affecting my lungs during practice."

As soon as Coach Eastman pulls into the parking lot, we run in to tell our fathers. We've been keeping a lookout so that they can speak to him alone.

"Okay, now you boys go and change." Dad points me in the direction of the dressing rooms.

When I round the corner to the hall leading to the dressing rooms, I stop. "Let's not go yet. I want to hear what they say. After all, it's going to affect me."

We sit on our hockey bags, straining our ears to hear.

"Hi, Mr. Rivers. How is Lee?" we hear Coach Eastman say pleasantly.

"He's fine. That's what we want to talk to you about," Dad says. "My son really enjoys playing hockey but there are times when his asthma acts up. I was wondering if we could work something out."

"You really should talk to Doug Hartford —"

"No point in it. That man doesn't listen," Mr. Thunderchild interrupts. "Look, Coach, do you think Lee should be penalized for his illness?"

"Well no…"

"So what can you do to make it better for him?" Ryan's dad asks.

"Well…I suppose he could do as much as his health lets him at practice. But while he's on the ice he has to give it all he's got."

"That sounds fair," Dad says.

ALL RIGHT. No problem, I think.

"Are you kidding?" Mr. Hartford must have shown up. His voice booms in the clubhouse. "Rob, think a minute. We can't be seen playing favourites, you know."

"Then let up on all the boys. It isn't necessary to be so hard on them," Ryan's father says.

"Just let the kids play. What do you say, Mr. Eastman?" Dad asks the coach.

"Well…" Eastman hesitates. "I think we need *some* consequences, but perhaps we can ease up a bit —"

"No way! Rob, are you going to let these jellyfish tell us how to run our team? We've got the playoffs to prepare for. These kids need conditioning if we're to make any kind of a showing in them," Hartford's loud angry voice reaches the hall.

"Does that really matter, Coach? What about the goals that *you* set at the start of the season?" Dad asks.

"Um, ah… I think —"

"Rob, stop letting these turkeys put you on the spot. You two should stop bullying the coach," Mr. Hartford growls.

"Bullying? Who's the one that's telling the coach what to do?" Ryan's dad bursts out laughing. "We were having a civilized conversation until you showed up."

"Well you're not following the protocol set up at the beginning."

"We would if you listened to our concerns. I've tried a number of times but you just blow me off," Mr. Thunderchild snaps.

"Besides it's your style of coaching that we have problems with," my father says.

"No one else does. Do they, Rob? Have you had any complaints?"

"How would he know? You won't let anyone near him."

"Now, Mr. Thunderchild, I'm sure that's not true." Coach Eastman shakes his head.

"Isn't it, Coach? The last time I tried to speak to you, he shooed you out and took over. He's taken over the team — can't you see that?" Ryan's dad asks.

"You're exaggerating." The coach refuses to believe them.

"No, he's not," Dad argues with the coach. "Ever since he started helping you coach, you've pushed the kids too hard and benched them for things they have no control over."

"I get the job done. If your wussy kids can't handle the pace, sign them up with the girls for ringette. I've taken this team from the near the bottom to the third from the top. They're going to win the playoffs or I'll die trying," the ogre snarls.

"What you really mean is *or they'll die trying*. For heaven's sake winning isn't everything. Especially not at the expense of a kid's health. This is only recreational hockey, for crying out loud." Dad is ticked.

"That's all right for you to say. Your kid's a lousy player. Mick isn't. He's lost a year playing with these jokers. The Saint Boniface and Saint Vital coaches were so stupid they all cut him. Well, there are plenty of coaches that know a good thing when they see it and I plan on getting him where he'll be seen — the city playoffs. Thunderchild, you should be thanking me instead of whining. Your son's in the same boat. Come on Eastman, we've got a practice to run."

At the sound of footsteps heading in our direction, Ryan and I grab our bags and scramble for the dressing room. The loud voices follow us.

"My son is happy where he's playing," Mr. Thunderchild calls down the hall.

"Yeah, right. Don't tell me he has no ambitions for the NHL?" Mr. Hartford yells back from the dressing room door.

"Get real, there's more to life than hockey. Besides he's only eleven. Time enough yet to catch the scout's eye," Mr. Thunderchild's voice penetrates the room before the door slams shut.

I remember the Triple A coaches talking to Coach Eastman. "You're already being scouted," I say to Ryan and tell him what I heard. His chocolate eyes sparkle and a grin as wide as an open net, spreads across his face.

"What was that all about?" Scott whispers.

"Dad was trying to arrange something with the coaches so I wouldn't have to quit because of my asthma," I whisper back.

" All that yelling and screaming, I am thinking that it did not work," Ashok comments quietly.

'No kidding," I answer.

"What are you guys staring at?" Mr. Hartford glares at the team. All eyes have been focused on him since he slammed the door. The hulk's eyes light on me and my friends. "Why aren't you changed? Get moving or you'll be benched."

I change faster than I've ever done before and manage to be on the rink before Mr. Hartford blows his whistle for the laps. Even though it's much warmer today, I decide to pace myself with Scott. Finishing the man-makers without stopping, is my goal. I take nice even strokes, enjoying the clean crisp air. I feel someone on my heels so I slow to let them pass.

"This isn't a stroll through the park, Rivers. Pick up your pace." Mr. Hartford falls in behind me — so close that I have to speed up to avoid being trampled. He speeds up too. We keep up this dance until he is satisfied that I'm moving at an acceptable pace. He follows me through the man-makers, too. My pace is much faster than I want it to be. By the end there's an ape on my chest again, but it's not King Kong, maybe only his baby. If I go for my inhaler I know I'll be okay.

"Where do you think you're going?" Mr. Hartford snaps at me.

"I need my inhaler."

"Leave the rink and you'll pay for it in ice time," he warns.

I stare him straight in the eye for a moment, then turn and walk off the ice.

As soon as the medication has worked I return. I couldn't have been gone more than ten minutes, but Hartford is waiting for me at the gate. "Go change. There's no point in you coming back. There's not enough time left to do anything. You and your father have pretty well wasted this practice. And don't bother coming to the next game because, once again, you didn't complete either of the practices this week."

Dad comes up to me as I head back into the clubhouse. "What's up, buddy?"

When I tell him, he is furious. He paces the floor while I change. I can almost feel the anger bubbling inside of him. We wait for the practice to end and he corners Coach Eastman in the hall.

"What do you want from this kid? You say you don't want to jeopardize his health, but you let Hartford dog him during practice. Now he has to sit out a game because he went in to use his puffer. Would you have preferred him to have another attack like last time — one that sends him to the hospital?"

"I'm sorry, Mr. Rivers, but there's not much I can do. I'd like to cut your son some slack but the rules aren't mine." Coach Eastman's face is beet red and he's staring at the floor as he speaks.

"Good heaven's, man, aren't you the head coach? Why are you letting that oaf dictate what you can do?"

"Well…since he's been helping, the team has been winning. I really think he knows what he's doing. The club's board is impressed with our progress. I'm sorry it hasn't worked out for your son —"

"You know what? I don't think you are sorry. You're gutless and hiding behind Hartford. You are just as happy to win as he is. And, if it means that you have to break a little boy's heart along the way, too bad. People like you are as much to blame for ruining recreational hockey as the Hartfords of this world." Dad doesn't wait for an answer. He just strides out of the building and I run to catch up.

12

For the Love of the Game

Pawtuxet Valley Daily Times
Saturday, October 3, 1964
...The latest addition to the Reds' hockey shrine (Rhode Island Reds Hall of Fame) *includes.... Gus Rivers.... The smooth skating forward was with the Roosters for five years, too. After several seasons with the Montreal Canadiens, Rivers came to Providence to stay. In 1934–35 he was among the CAN-AM scoring leaders...*

April 3, 1932
Dear Stan,
Well, you win some — you lose some. Can't get greedy. Lou Pieri spoke to me again after our last game with Boston. He's keen on me joining his club, the Rhode Island Reds, next season. Guarantees me a spot on the first string and the same dough I'm making with Montreal. You know how much I want to play so, how can I turn down a great deal like that? I feel like kicking up my heels.

Gus

I'm spending the night at Grandpa's because my parents are staying out late. Boy am I glad. They've been insisting all week that I have to quit hockey and for some crazy reason I've been fighting them. I've already made up my mind to split the Jets. I guess I'm just not ready to say it yet.

The way I figure it, watching the game from the stands is the same as not being on the team at all. And that's where I'll be, if I don't complete the practices. With Hartford on my case — pushing me — making sure I can't, there is no point in hanging on.

As always, I find myself drawn to the den, but this time there is a queasy feeling in my tummy. Would The Uncles understand?

I open the cedar chest. Uncle Romie's smiling face stares up at me. It looks like he's laughing silently. Is he laughing at sickly old me for trying to follow in their footsteps? I turn the picture over to hide his face. I take out the hockey photos and spread them out around me. I'm never going to be the next great Rivers. I can't even play. I envied my friend's health.

"Why so glum?" Grandpa sits down beside me.

I tell him about my shattered dreams.

"Does being famous mean so much to you?" he asks.

"It's not about being famous; I just wanted to be like them. But now all I want to do is play the game."

A big smile spreads across Grandpa's face. "Then you are like them. They played for the love of the game, too. When the NHL came calling the only one to bite was Uncle Gus. The others turned them down and kept playing in Winnipeg. And even Uncle Gus, after winning two Stanley Cups, left the Canadiens to play hockey."

"That doesn't make sense," I say.

"Yes, it does. You see, Montreal had such a strong team that it would have taken years to move in the lineup. So when the Rhode Island Reds offered him a place on their starting line, he took it, because *he* just wanted to play. So don't give up yet, Lee. There are other teams. Other coaches."

He's right. I pick up the snapshots and put them back in the cedar chest. Before I shut it I turn over Uncle Romie's photo. This time his smile isn't mocking me. I've made my peace with The Uncles. I can now tell the world.

* * *

"You're really quitting?" Scott eyes are as wide as an open net.

I nod. I turn Uncle Romie's Olympic gold medal in my hands. Grandpa let me bring some things home to show my friends.

"I do not understand. You are liking hockey so much." Ashok shakes his head and reaches for the object in my hand.

"I'm just quitting the Jets, not giving up on hockey," I say.

"I wouldn't quit. I'd stay just to bug Hartford, like a burr under his saddle." Ryan grins and hands Scott Uncle Joe's World Cup medal.

"That would be funny, but he's just not worth having asthma attacks over," I say.

"It's so not fair, that you have to quit because of that jerk." Scott shakes his head.

"Don't worry, I'll find a way back next year. Maybe there will be other coaches."

"One thing for sure, Hartford won't be there. You heard what he said. He's determined to have Mick play Triple A."

"See, things are already looking better. Until then, I'll practise in my backyard."

"I most certainly will be missing you." Ashok's forehead is creased in a frown.

"Why? We're still friends. The four of us can continue playing hockey on my rink."

"Oh, yes. How silly of me." Ashok hits his forehead with his palm and giggles.

Ryan picks up and examines a photo of me that is sitting on my dresser.

"Where is this?" he says, tapping the photo.

"Lac du Bonnet. It's our family cottage. The Uncles and their brothers built the cabin themselves."

"It looks like a good place to be."

"It's great. Maybe we can all go there sometime. It's boat access only. Grandpa likes to say that there's nothing but bush between our cabin and the North Pole. I don't think it's true but I stay out of it. I'm afraid of getting lost in the wild."

"I wouldn't be afraid. I miss the bush. I love the smells. Pine. Wet earthy leaves. Chokecherry blossoms. Grandfather used to take me and Uncle Johnny camping in the bush. We'd find a nice high spot to set up the tent. Mostly we would live off the land. Grandfather would say, 'Washmakwa, the earth —"

"Washmawhat?"

"Washmakwa. Grandfather always calls me by my native name. It means white bear. Anyway, he would say that the earth provides a vast feast for her people, but modern man's tastes are so narrow. He showed us what plants we could eat. Some even tasted good."

"Like what?" I asked.

"Mushrooms, saskatoons and other berries of course, but the soft bottom end of cattails are good, too. Boiled and smothered in butter. That's yummy. Once we forgot the tea bags so Grandfather took us to a low-lying area to pick Labrador tea. It tasted musty but okay. The leaves are strange — green and smooth on top and brown velvet, like a deer's ear, on the bottom."

"No offense, but yuck, I'd rather starve. I'm not crazy about

the vegetables that Mom gets from the store. I like my meat."
Scott looks like he sucked on a lemon.

"Meat we had. Not the stuff you'd get in the grocery store.
Johnny was good at snaring rabbits. Or if it was hunting season
and we bagged a partridge or deer we'd eat that. Otherwise
there was always fish. Grandfather brought an old rack from a
barbecue to put over the open fire and we'd grill the meat.
Nothing ever tasted so good. Dad says maybe I can go back for
the summer. I hope so."

When my friends leave, I wander into the family room looking for company. Dad's sitting in the leather recliner reading a
letter. Mom's sitting on the arm, reading over his shoulder. They
don't hear me coming.

"What do you think? Should we let Lee?" Dad waves the
letter.

"If it was from anyone else, I'd say no right off the bat."
Mom points to the bottom of the piece of paper. "But, him I
trust. We can reason with him. It's all indoors, too."

"What's indoors? And who do you trust?" I startle them.

Dad grabs Mom and pulls her into his lap to keep her from
falling off the arm.

"Don't sneak up on us like that," she says, giggling.

"We could be kissing, you know," laughs Dad.

"Oh, gross." I stick my finger in my open mouth and make
a gagging sound. "What was that you were reading? Tell me."

"Here, read for yourself." Dad hands me the letter.

"Dear Mr. and Mrs. Rivers," I read out aloud. "Myself and a
number of like-minded people are in the process of setting up a
spring hockey league based on Fair Play rules. The object of the
league is to have fun while developing good hockey skills. Each
week there will be a half-hour skills' building session followed by
a game. All sessions will be held at the Highlander complex.

We are now at the stage of recruiting players. During my time with the John Forsyth Jets, I noticed a number of players were getting shortchanged in their hockey experience. I think they would enjoy our program. As I will be coaching one of the teams, I am sending letters to these kids. I had the pleasure of coaching your son while I was with the Jets and thought he might be interested. If he is, contact me at 555-3247. Regards, Brent Jenkins."

"Well?" My parents look at me expectantly.

"Would I? As fast as Al MacInnis can shoot!"

Canadian Pacific Steamship Lines
R.M.S. S.S. Montrose
December 1, 1934
Dear Gang,
...You can give mamma and papa our love and tell them that we are having a swell time. We will be on the ice Monday morning (Dec. 3). From then on everything will be pleasant...
Goodbye

Joe & Romie

Other books you'll enjoy in the Sports Stories series...

Baseball

❏ *Curve Ball* by John Danakas #1
Tom Poulos is looking forward to a summer of baseball in Toronto until his mother puts him on a plane to Winnipeg.

❏ *Baseball Crazy* by Martyn Godfrey #10
Rob Carter wins an all-expenses-paid chance to be bat boy at the Blue Jays spring training camp in Florida.

❏ *Shark Attack* by Judi Peers #25
The East City Sharks have a good chance of winning the county championship until their arch rivals get a tough new pitcher.

❏ *Hit and Run* by Dawn Hunter and Karen Hunter #35
Glen Thomson is a talented pitcher, but as his ego inflates, team morale plummets. Will he learn from being benched for losing his temper?

❏ *Power Hitter* by C. A. Forsyth #41
Connor's summer was looking like a write-off. That is, until he discovered his secret talent.

❏ *Sayonara, Sharks* by Judi Peers #48
In this sequel to *Shark Attack*, Ben and Kate are excited about the school trip to Japan, but Matt's not sure he wants to go.

Basketball

❏ *Fast Break* by Michael Coldwell #8
Moving from Toronto to small-town Nova Scotia was rough, but when Jeff makes the school basketball team he thinks things are looking up.

❏ *Camp All-Star* by Michael Coldwell #12
In this insider's view of a basketball camp, Jeff Lang encounters some unexpected challenges.

❏ *Nothing but Net* by Michael Coldwell #18
The Cape Breton Grizzly Bears prepare for an out-of-town basketball tournament they're sure to lose.

❑ *Slam Dunk* by Steven Barwin and Gabriel David Tick #23
In this sequel to *Roller Hockey Blues*, Mason Ashbury's basketball team adjusts to the arrival of some new players: girls.

❑ *Courage on the Line* by Cynthia Bates #33
After Amelie changes schools, she must confront difficult former teammates in an extramural match.

❑ *Free Throw* by Jacqueline Guest #34
Matthew Eagletail must adjust to a new school, a new team and a new father along with five pesky sisters.

❑ *Triple Threat* by Jacqueline Guest #38
Matthew's cyber-pal Free Throw comes to visit, and together they face a bully on the court.

❑ *Queen of the Court* by Michele Martin Bossley #40
What happens when the school's fashion queen winds up on the basketball court?

❑ *Shooting Star* by Cynthia Bates #46
Quyen is dealing with a troublesome teammate on her new basketball team, as well as trouble at home. Her parents seem haunted by something that happened in Vietnam.

❑ *Home Court Advantage* by Sandra Diersch #51
Debbie had given up hope of being adopted, until the Lowells came along. Things were looking up, until Debbie is accused of stealing from the team.

❑ *Rebound* by Adrienne Mercer #54
C.J.'s dream in life is to play on the national basketball team. But one day she wakes up in pain and can barely move her joints, much less be a star player.

Figure Skating

❑ *A Stroke of Luck* by Kathryn Ellis #6
Strange accidents are stalking one of the skaters at the Millwood Arena.

❑ *The Winning Edge* by Michele Martin Bossley #28
Jennie wants more than anything to win a gruelling series of competitions, but is success worth losing her friends?

❑ *Leap of Faith* by Michele Martin Bossley #36
Amy wants to win at any cost, until an injury makes skating almost impossible. Will she go on?

Gymnastics

❑ *The Perfect Gymnast* by Michele Martin Bossley #9
Abby's new friend has all the confidence she needs, but she also has a serious problem that nobody but Abby seems to know about.

Ice Hockey

❑ *Two Minutes for Roughing* by Joseph Romain #2
As a new player on a tough Toronto hockey team, Les must fight to fit in.

❑ *Hockey Night in Transcona* by John Danakas #7
Cody Powell gets promoted to the Transcona Sharks' first line, bumping out the coach's son, who's not happy with the change.

❑ *Face Off* by C. A. Forsyth #13
A talented hockey player finds himself competing with his best friend for a spot on a select team.

❑ *Hat Trick* by Jacqueline Guest #20
The only girl on an all-boy hockey team works to earn the captain's respect and her mother's approval.

❑ *Hockey Heroes* by John Danakas #22
A left-winger on the thirteen-year-old Transcona Sharks adjusts to a new best friend and his mom's boyfriend.

❑ *Hockey Heat Wave* by C. A. Forsyth #27
In this sequel to *Face Off*, Zack and Mitch run into trouble when it looks as if only one of them will make the select team at hockey camp.

❑ *Shoot to Score* by Sandra Richmond #31
Playing defense on the B list alongside the coach's mean-spirited son is a tough obstacle for Steven to overcome, but he perseveres and changes his luck.

❑ *Rookie Season* by Jacqueline Guest #42
What happens when a boy wants to join an all-girl hockey team?

❏ *Brothers on Ice* by John Danakas #44
Brothers Dylan and Deke both want to play goal for the same team.

❏ *Rink Rivals* by Jacqueline Guest #49
A move to Calgary finds the Evans twins pitted against each other on the ice, and struggling to help each other out of trouble.

❏ *Power Play* by Michele Martin Bossley #50
An early-season injury causes Zach Thomas to play timidly, and a school bully just makes matters worse. Will a famous hockey player will be able to help Zach sort things out?

Riding

❏ *A Way with Horses* by Peter McPhee #11
A young Alberta rider, invited to study show jumping at a posh local riding school, uncovers a secret.

❏ *Riding Scared* by Marion Crook #15
A reluctant new rider struggles to overcome her fear of horses.

❏ *Katie's Midnight Ride* by C. A. Forsyth #16
An ambitious barrel racer finds herself without a horse weeks before her biggest rodeo.

❏ *Glory Ride* by Tamara L. Williams #21
Chloe Anderson fights memories of a tragic fall for a place on the Ontario Young Riders Team.

❏ *Cutting It Close* by Marion Crook #24
In this novel about barrel racing, a young rider finds her horse is in trouble just as she's about to compete in an important event.

❏ *Shadow Ride* by Tamara L. Williams #37
Bronwen has to choose between competing aggressively for herself or helping out a teammate.

Roller Hockey

❏ *Roller Hockey Blues* by Steven Barwin and Gabriel David Tick #17
Mason Ashbury faces a summer of boredom until he makes the roller hockey team.

Running

❏ *Fast Finish* by Bill Swan #30
Noah is a promising young runner headed for the provincial finals when he suddenly decides to withdraw from the event.

Sailing

❏ *Sink or Swim* by William Pasnak #5
Dario can barely manage the dog paddle, but thanks to his mother he's spending the summer at a water sports camp.

Soccer

❏ *Lizzie's Soccer Showdown* by John Danakas #3
When Lizzie asks why the boys and girls can't play together, she finds herself the new captain of the soccer team.

❏ *Alecia's Challenge* by Sandra Diersch #32
Thirteen-year-old Alecia has to cope with a new school, a new step-father, and friends who have suddenly discovered the opposite sex.

❏ *Shut-Out!* by Camilla Reghelini Rivers #39
David wants to play soccer more than anything, but will the new coach let him?

❏ *Offside!* by Sandra Diersch #43
Alecia has to confront a new girl who drives her teammates crazy.

❏ *Heads Up!* by Dawn Hunter and Karen Hunter #45
Do the Warriors really need a new, hot-shot player who skips practice?

❏ *Off the Wall* by Camilla Reghelini Rivers #52
Lizzie loves indoor soccer, and she's thrilled when her little sister gets into the sport. But when their teams are pitted against each other, Lizzie can only warn her sister to watch out.

❏ *Trapped!* by Michele Martin Bossley #53
There's a thief on Jane's soccer team, and everyone thinks it's her best friend, Ashley. Jane must find the true culprit to save both Ashley and the team's morale.

Swimming

❏ *Breathing Not Required* by Michele Martin Bossley #4
Gracie works so hard to be chosen for the solo at synchronized swimming that she almost loses her best friend in the process.

❏ *Water Fight!* by Michele Martin Bossley #14
Josie's perfect sister is driving her crazy, but when she takes up swimming — Josie's sport — it's too much to take.

❏ *Taking a Dive* by Michele Martin Bossley #19
Josie holds the provincial record for the butterfly, but in this sequel to Water Fight! she can't seem to match her own time and might not go on to the nationals.

❏ *Great Lengths* by Sandra Diersch #26
Fourteen-year-old Jessie decides to find out whether the rumours about a new swimmer at her Vancouver club are true.

❏ *Pool Princess* by Michele Martin Bossley #47
In this sequel to *Breathing Not Required*, Gracie must deal with a bully on the new synchro team in Calgary.

Track and Field

❏ *Mikayla's Victory* by Cynthia Bates #29
Mikayla must compete against her friend if she wants to represent her school at an important track event.

❏ *Walker's Runners* by Robert Rayner #55
Toby Morton hates gym. In fact, he doesn't run for anything — except the classroom door. Then Mr. Walker arrives and persuades Toby to join the running team.